Drowning.

Jessie waited a breathless moment for the girl to surface as she had the last time. But just when she thought she saw the surfboard bobbing up without the surfer, a huge wave came crashing ashore, burying it. The wave washed halfway up the beach, erasing Jessie's footprints in one fell swoop as well as any sign of life from the stranger. . . .

**Other Thrillers
you will enjoy:**

THE SURFER

LINDA CARGILL

SCHOLASTIC INC.
New York Toronto London Auckland Sydney

No part of this publication may be reproduced in whole or in part, or stored in a retrieval system, or transmitted in any form or by any means, electronic, mechanical, photocopying, recording, or otherwise, without written permission of the publisher. For information regarding permission, write to Scholastic Inc., 555 Broadway, New York, NY 10012.

ISBN 0-590-22215-5

12 11 10 9 8 7 6 5 4 3 2 1   5 6 7 8 9/9 0/0

Printed in the U.S.A.   01

First Scholastic printing, July 1995

To Mr. Key, who was with me in spirit the whole way.

THE SURFER

Chapter 1

Dear Diary:

I'm grounded again. Mom just won't quit. All she does is nag, nag, nag. If it's not, "Jessie, haven't you gotten your hair cut yet?" it's, "I think you'd better go on a diet. You're not twelve years old anymore. You're seventeen. You should look like a young lady."

But that's not what got me sent to my bedroom today. It's, "Why can't you stop daydreaming? Lately you're acting like your mind's somewhere else."

I wish Mom were my friend and not my enemy. But then I guess she's got too many problems of her own right now. And Dad, too. He finally moved out last week. Just packed his bags and left. The divorce is supposed to be final in six months.

I really wish I had somebody to talk to. I wish

I could tell her about it — you know, Diary, all about what only you know. What's been happening to me.

I guess I could tell Nick, but he's a guy. And you know how guys are. Sometimes they're good listeners, but Nick says when he goes to sleep at night he just conks out. He doesn't even remember his dreams. When we have parties and try to scare each other with stories, he keeps his mouth shut. It gets worse. Sometimes I even have to elbow him in the ribs because he just falls asleep. He says he's tired from all that swimming he does for the team, but I think he's just bored.

Trish would probably listen, but she's such a cynic. The last thing I want is to be the butt of one of her jokes. I can just hear her now: "You keep drowning in your dreams? Ridiculous. Sounds like indigestion to me."

Besides, I'm not trying to scare anybody. This is very real and kind of weird. Almost every night now, I fall asleep as soon as I shut my eyes. I used to drift off gradually, thinking about everything I did during the day. But now I can't help myself. Even when I don't feel really tired, all I have to do is shut my eyes and I'm dragged off by some undertow — like in the ocean. I can't catch my breath. Something heavy, dark,

2

and black presses down on my lungs, and I can't breathe. It fills my mouth, and I can't speak. It even covers my eyes so I can't see. I flail about hopelessly. Just when my lungs are ready to burst, I wake up gasping. It feels as if I've been swimming upward and have just broken the surface of the water. My nightgown is always bathed in sweat.

You know, Diary, I've been on the swim team since I was in ninth grade. I'm nothing great. Average time and all. But I've never been afraid of the water. What's wrong with me? I'm going to go crazy if this doesn't stop soon.

Jessie got into her car and zoomed away from the house. She was able to nudge her old Buick into one of the few parking spaces next to the boardwalk at Atlantic and 36th Streets — the only luck she'd had lately. But then it was May, a few weeks before the tourist season started in earnest.

As she crossed the grassy area in front of the ice cream store, she passed a statue. Everyone in Virginia Beach called it "The Norwegian Lady." This nine-foot bronze sculpture was supposed to watch over all those who went out to sea. It reminded Jessie of her fourth-grade field trip, when the teacher told the class the monument had been a gift to Virginia Beach from the people of Norway. The statue commemorated the tragic wreck of the ship *The Norwegian Lady*. The date etched in bronze read "1897."

The Norwegian Lady kept her eyes fixed on the far distance, the horizon, where the sky met the sea.

Jessie had to wait beside the monument for the boardwalk train to pass, taking passengers from their hotel rooms to restaurants and amusement parks. A little boy carrying a pink plastic miniature golf club rode on it. People didn't even seem to notice The Norwegian Lady as they walked up and down the board-walk with their packages, hurrying to lunch, to a business appointment, or just because they were double-parked.

People sort of got used to the statue's face after a while. Jessie noticed the statue, she thought, because she was feeling rather glum. That's when she heard a voice.

"Hey, Jess, where are you going?" Nick said. Jessie looked up with a start at six feet of lanky bones and muscles. It was only Nick sporting his tousled head of red hair.

He was always surprising her like that, showing up everywhere. They'd known each other since they were kids, but she thought Nick presumed too much. Sometimes she thought he was following her around. Just because he was a senior and she was only a junior, he thought he was all grown up and sort of like a big brother.

"Look, Nick, I'm busy now. All right?" She shrugged him off.

But he soon caught up with her. "Wait a minute, Jess! I just asked you where you are going."

"Go ahead and tell my parents, why don't you? You're good at *that.*" Jessie walked as fast as she could, keeping to the far side of the boardwalk, closest to the sea. She shoved her hands into the pockets of her green blazer and kept her head down, looking at her sneakers.

"Look, Jess, you know that wasn't my fault," Nick kept up easily with her. His legs were so long they were almost out of proportion with the rest of him. That's probably why he was the lead breaststroker on the swim team. "You hadn't checked in with your mom after school, and she called me. I had to tell her you were going to the beach. I mean — "

"You mean, you're just a snitch!" She turned around and glared at him. "You don't want to give me any space — just like my mother and everybody else."

"Now, Jess, you know that's not fair. *You* told me where you were going. I thought there was something wrong." He shrugged. "Maybe something happened to you — or something."

"Well, Mr. Olympic Breaststroker, for your information, I've been on the swim team three years, and I can swim just as well as you can. I can also take care of myself."

"You're going to the beach again?"

"What of it?"

"Nothing, except . . . well, you know. The police have asked people to stay away from the old fishing pier. You remember the drownings in April? They've got buoys and lines up everywhere. Some old plankings are loose or something."

"Oh, stop acting like an old woman and leave me alone!" She stalked off.

The old fishing pier was her favorite place. It always had been. Ever since she had gotten a car when she was a sophomore, it had been her hideaway, her special spot to be alone where it was quiet and she could think.

As soon as Jessie reached the stairs leading down to the beach, she took them two at a time and then kicked off her sneakers. She ran through the sand in her bare feet. It felt warm to the touch. It was the middle of May, just a couple of weeks before the beginning of the tourist season on Memorial Day weekend. The weather had been unusually chilly this spring, and she longed like crazy for the first hot days of summer. She could come here every day then after she got off her job at the swimming pool where she worked as a lifeguard.

Just as she always did, Jessie ran down to the water's edge and let the waves lap up over her feet until they were buried in the sand. At first the water felt very chilly indeed, but she soon got used to it.

Jessie looked out to sea. She saw those annoying red buoys. Everybody had to act like an old grandmother these days just because a couple of silly boys had been killed playing around the old pier after dark. Their heads had been smashed in as if someone hit them with boards or rocks. They could have gotten drunk, beat each other up, and then fallen off the pier to be washed up on the rocks. Jessie was certainly not about to do anything so silly herself.

She climbed up on the pile of rocks between the pier and what used to be the inlet to an old bay. Now everyone used Rudee Inlet, several miles up the beach by the lighthouse. When she stood on her tiptoes and squinted she could barely make it out in the distance, along with all the fishing boats, deep sea charters, tour boats, and private yachts that went in and out all day long.

Jessie felt herself falling. Instinctively she put out her hands to cushion her landing on the jagged granite blocks. But she seemed to fall harder than she expected. The strength in her hands did not prevent her from scraping her knee badly and bruising her elbow so that it turned black and blue. She said, "Oh, darn!" and took out a pocket handkerchief to tie around her bleeding knee.

She didn't know what had come over her. Usually she could keep her balance anywhere. Maybe it was all the excitement lately. She certainly was not going to let the experience unnerve her. Jessie was going to go about her day as she always did.

Jessie clambered down from the rocks more carefully than she had climbed up and started up the rickety wooden steps of the old pier. She paused halfway up, feeling a sweat start under her arms. "This is silly!" she said aloud. "Now you're acting like a jerk, Jess." But she had suffered from sudden premonitions all her life. For a moment she was breathless, thinking she felt a cold finger touching the back of her neck. Her heart started pounding, and she felt giddy. It was all she could do to hold on tight to the railing, digging her fingernails into the old wood.

Jessie took a deep breath for courage and spun around. There was no one behind her, of course. Only a cold droplet of sweat streamed down the back of her neck. She realized that's what it was all along — just droplets of sweat. No one had really touched her.

"This is the outside of too much!" Jessie groaned, trying to laugh at herself. She kept climbing the steps, tossing her hair back over her shoulders to get it out of her eyes.

Now that she was up on the pier she was going to walk down to the end the way she always did, careful not to step on the cracks for fear of bad luck. There were old wooden buckets lying about, left there by fishermen of long ago — old crates that once smelled of fish. There was a new fishing pier a couple of miles down the beach in the opposite direction from the lighthouse. She had often gone there with Nick to catch dinner on rented fishing poles. But this was her private place.

She sat down on the end of the pier, dangling

her feet over the edge. This was more like old times with the wind blowing in her face and the sun beating down on her head.

Jessie had come here nearly every day after school for the past couple of years in the spring, the fall, and all during the long, hot summer. All winter long she would wait impatiently for the season to change, and on a warm day during the January thaw she could often be found strolling on the beach or sitting on the old pier. The sea drew her to it.

She felt on top of the world here. Nothing could go wrong. She could see for miles and miles. Jessie could sit so still that a seagull would often wing by and land right next to her on top of a wooden railing or a mooring pole stuck into the sea.

A flick of the switch turned her Walkman on. The music calmed her. No one here could yell at her for flunking her latest geometry test. Her father couldn't tell her she was a disgrace to the family and that she would never amount to anything. The seagulls were glad for the pocketful of bread crumbs she had brought from the school cafeteria. They seemed to like her just for being herself.

Jessie was sitting on the pier looking out to sea thinking how much nicer it was when her parents used to bring her here as a child. Then she spotted something far out on the water. At first she could not make it out clearly. Was it a leaping dolphin? It was too large for that, but not so large as a ship or a boat.

Whatever it was, it was moving toward shore. And it was moving rapidly.

Jessie stood up. It looked like a person, a girl on a surfboard. Jessie had been surfing a few times herself and wondered how the girl, whoever she was, could have started so far out at sea that she seemed like a speck on the horizon. The surf did not begin to break, and the waves did not form, until they reached the sandbars. The sandbars were closer to the beach. Everybody knew that.

But Jessie only knew what she saw. There was no doubt about it now. The figure was definitely a girl in a red, one-piece bathing suit. Her long, blond hair streamed out behind her in the wind like a flag, and she possessed the most striking, beautiful white skin Jessie had ever seen. The surfboard was tethered to her ankle the way all surfers did it, but it was odd that she didn't have a wet suit. It still was kind of chilly in May to go so far out in only a bathing suit. The water temperature must still be in the upper sixties.

Soon Jessie's doubts were swallowed up in her admiration for the stranger's acrobatics. She seemed to be just catching the peak of a very long, cresting wave. She was planing with perfect balance, her knees bent just so and her long, slender arms thrust out to either side. The pose was so perfect and so effortlessly sustained that Jessie found herself imitating the girl on the surfboard, bending her own knees as she stood on the edge of the old pier. Only at the last moment did she remember to move back.

As if that perfect balance was not enough for such an expert surfer, the girl now lifted one leg up from the board and rode the cresting wave with only one knee bent. And then, incredibly, she thrust that leg out behind her, balancing herself first on her hands and then again on one foot. It was as if the stranger were a ballerina who could walk and dance on water! Jessie heard herself gasp and put her hands over her mouth.

The stranger looked up just where Jessie was standing, almost as if she could hear Jessie. That was impossible because she was so far away. The girl did not look at all surprised or put off by all the police buoys. She merely smiled, curling her red lips upward, and waved at Jessie.

For a moment, Jessie felt confused. She did not know why. It was perfectly natural to be friendly, except that almost no one had the skill to wave from a surfboard without falling. Shyly, she waved back.

Jessie was surprised not merely by the girl's skill but by her looks. The stranger was clearly a raving beauty. She seemed about Jessie's age, but it was hard to tell for sure. She looked so grown up in that bathing suit, just like a contestant in a Miss America contest. She might be tall, but there was not an ounce of spare flesh on her body. Everything was all muscle, in the right places — and curves, in the right places, too.

Just gazing at the girl made Jessie feel awkward. She was too average-looking herself, she guessed. Nobody ever noticed her in a crowd. In a movie theater there were just as many heads above hers blocking her view as below. She became tall enough to ride the roller coasters at the amusement park at just the same age as most everybody else. When she complained to her friend Trish, who was the tallest girl in the class, Trish smirked and said, "Would you rather be a Frankenstein like me?"

With her curly brown hair and hazel eyes Jessie knew she couldn't compete with this stranger with the striking blond hair and white complexion. Even worse, all Jessie could think of was her mother saying, "My, you've been putting on some weight lately!" How could she explain to Mother that there was nothing to do but raid the refrigerator when she was afraid to sleep at night?

The stranger on the surfboard seemed to be putting on a show now that she knew that Jessie was standing there watching her. She stood on one foot again, even on tiptoe, and then in a flash flipped over onto her head, holding on to the board with both hands. This was something else Jessie had never seen before and never thought possible. Jessie clapped.

The extraordinarily long wave finally gave out. The girl went under only to surface again. She immediately scooted herself up on her surfboard belly first and waved once more at Jessie.

Jessie thought it would be only polite to introduce herself. "My name's Jessie, Jessie Rogers," she cupped her hands and called at the top of her lungs. The girl was barely within hailing distance. "You look like a pretty tough customer out there on that board."

"Thanks!" the girl called back, smiling. "Do you want to see some more?"

The girl moved so fast that Jessie did not even have a chance to answer. She used her hands to dig down into the waves and push her board farther out to sea. Her shoulder muscles gave her strength to fight the frothing tops of the waves. The onshore wind was picking up quite a bit.

"Hey!" Jessie called after the girl. "Are you sure you want to go out there again? It looks like it might rain." The sky was clouding up with dark blue and black clouds. They were big and puffy, just the sort of thing one expected before a storm.

"I like the water," came the answer. Jessie barely heard it. She couldn't even be sure the girl had said it. She was turned in the other direction, and in this weather the words didn't make much sense.

A jagged lightning bolt hit the water far out at sea.

Great! thought Jessie. *Just great. Now it's all my fault. I encouraged her.*

The stranger rose on her surfboard again.

The waves were bigger now. She seemed to be riding the hump of a ten-foot swell that was about ready to hit the sandbar and crest into a white, frothy peak. The sea had turned dark all around her, but still she put on her acrobatic show, riding on one foot, balancing on one hand, and even doing little leaps from one end of the board to the other.

Jessie put her hand to her throat in fear. Could she possibly make it?

The girl was closer now than she had been before on her first ride in. It looked as if she was coming in to shore, riding the wave perfectly all the way up the beach. She was near enough that Jessie could make out a necklace of shells from which hung a large, round crystal pendant with a blue turquoise center. The jewel was the same shade of blue as the girl's eyes. They were a limpid color and looked as pale as sunlight on the water. It seemed as if one could gaze into them forever and never reach the bottom. The girl's lips were pursed and turned up at the ends in a mysterious sort of smile. Her face was radiant. It gave off a glow. The stranger seemed to be confident of what she was doing — even if Jessie was not.

Then a horrible, unexpected thing happened. Just as Jessie was about to run down to the beach to greet her new acquaintance, the girl slipped off the board and with a terrible cry went under. It had to be impossible. The water was too shallow. She was almost ashore. But there was no denying the waves were fierce.

Jessie waited a breathless moment for the girl to surface as she had the last time. But just when she thought she saw the surfboard bobbing up without the surfer, a huge wave came crashing ashore, burying it. The wave washed halfway up the beach, erasing Jessie's footprints in one fell swoop as well as any sign of life from the stranger.

"Oh, no!" panicked Jessie. "She's hit her head. She'll be washed out to sea." Jessie just couldn't let that happen. She would be responsible.

Jessie took a deep breath and dove into the ocean from the pier. Soon she had a mouthful of seawater, but Jessie had taken lifesaving last summer and had performed a few rescues at the pool where she worked. She'd even on occasion made ocean rescues. She could not see well in the murky depths, but something bumped into her. It was solid and dense like a drifting human body. It seemed to coil its tentacles around her, and when Jessie grabbed a handful of them she saw it was human hair — blond hair.

Jessie hooked her arm under the girl's chin and tried to swim ashore. Although she could not see the girl, she felt it had to be her. Surely hers was the only body drifting around near the beach. It *had* to be her.

Jessie had swum in choppy waters before. But this was incredible. The sea had gone from rough — the kind of weather where a lifeguard put up a red flag for "dangerous surf" and told everyone with sense to get out of the water — to almost unswimmable. No one had predicted such a storm this morning when Jessie had heard the weather report. In fact, while she sat on the pier and dangled her legs she dimly remembered hearing something on the radio like "sunny skies, twenty percent chance of rain this afternoon. . . ." A storm of this magnitude did not just come out of nowhere.

The undertow was something fierce. Jessie was a strong swimmer, but she could hardly make any headway. She was so close to shore, and yet she could not reach it — kick and flail as she would. The girl's body seemed to be getting heavier and heavier. Jessie could barely hold on. But she just couldn't let go.

The girl would die, and she would be responsible.

Yet her fingers seemed to be losing their grip one by one. Something seemed to be tugging the girl in the other direction.

Jessie looked back over her shoulder in panic. The beach had been so close. It was getting farther and farther away. She, too, was being dragged out to sea.

As lightning flashed, a huge wave smashed over Jessie's head, pushing her away from the girl and sending them both down into the black waters of the frothing sea. Jessie felt she was being pulled every direction at once. Currents tugged down on her legs at the same time they tried to tear her arms out of their sockets. A wall of water had closed over her head, and she had been spun around so much she did not even know which way was up. She could see nothing but blackness everywhere.

Her lungs were going to burst if she didn't find some air soon. *I'm going to die!* was all she could think of, and then the memory of her dream hit her with the impact of another wave. Somehow she had known this was going to happen. She had lived it and relived it every night for weeks. But she had not listened. She had not known how to heed its warning. Jessie had not stayed away from the beach and the pier, and now because she hadn't she was going to die.

Oh, no, she wasn't! She tried to force herself to let her body go limp. She would float to the surface. But she was being knocked around too much for that to work. Nor could she see the direction of the bubbles. She had to take a wild guess which way was up. There was no time left before she would breathe in water.

With her last burst of strength she kicked, pushed, and clawed her way through the murky depths. Then suddenly someone grabbed Jessie around the waist. She hardly had the strength to resist, but she was being dragged the opposite direction from the way she had been swimming. Feebly she tried to peel the fingers away from her, but the grasp was like iron — strong and unyielding.

Finally they broke the surface. She could hardly catch her breath. She panted.

"Jessie, are you all right?" came a familiar voice.

It was Nick.

Chapter 2

"There's a girl out there in the water!" Jessie gasped. Now she remembered. They had to save her.

Nick didn't listen. He was intent only on pulling Jessie ashore through the turbulent waters. Jessie always teased him about his abilities as a breaststroker, but right now she was happy he was the best on the Virginia Beach High School swim team. She had not been able to make headway against the undertow, but with his arm looped protectively around her Nick was just keeping ahead of the tide. They were barely making it in.

Jessie had all she could do just to keep her head above the water. But she didn't feel right about leaving the scene, despite her own danger.

"Look, Nick, the storm's not so bad now.

It's letting up," she coughed as she pulled herself to her feet on the wet sand. "Please, let's go back and look for the girl. She might still be alive out there." Jessie pointed out to sea at the black waves, now rapidly brightening to their usual gray to gray-green color as the clouds blew away. The storm threatened to disappear as rapidly as it had come. From overhead a solitary ray of sunlight hit the sea.

Nick could do nothing but stare at her in amazement. Jessie was turning to run back into the water.

"Hold on there, Jess!" He grabbed her by the shoulders and spun her around to face him. "What in the hell are you doing? Are you out of your mind?"

Jessie was rapidly regaining her strength and shook herself free of Nick's grasp with a defiant toss of her head. "If you can call it a waste of time to save somebody's life!" She turned to go again.

"Now wait a minute, Jess! I'm no ax murderer. There's just no one out there."

"Of course there is. The girl — "

"What *girl?*"

"The tall one with the blond hair. You know" — she stomped her foot — "the one on the surfboard."

He wrinkled up his forehead and shook his head. "I was watching you the whole time from the boardwalk. I didn't see anybody but you."

"That's impossible!"

"I admit I thought you were nuts sitting on the pier talking to yourself while the storm rolled in. But I gave you the benefit of the doubt — that is, until you jumped in and tried to drown yourself."

So that's what you thought. . . . The hair stood up on the back of Jessie's neck in horror as the blood drained from her face.

How was it possible he didn't see the girl? She had been clearly visible. In fact, she was quite striking, not the sort of person you didn't notice. "You must at least have heard her speaking to me?" Jessie's voice sounded strained.

"Are you sure you feel OK?" Nick put his hand out to touch her forehead. He looked really concerned. "I mean, if there was a girl out there on a surfboard, we should at least see the board washed up on shore. Those things float, remember?"

Jessie shook her head and backed away from Nick. She didn't know what was going on here, but she didn't have time to argue. Not now when the girl could be dying. Jessie spotted passersby on the boardwalk. "Help!" she screamed. "Help! There's been a drowning. There's a girl lost at sea."

The kids on the boardwalk ran for help. "A drowning! A drowning!" they echoed as they scattered in all directions. They alarmed the hotel guests, who were just starting to come out of the hotel lobbies again after the storm to sun themselves beside the pools. One old lady burst into tears. Crowds started gathering at the railing of the boardwalk, gazing off into the ocean to see if they could make out any bodies. A policeman directing traffic on Atlantic Avenue, just behind the first string of hotels and motels, heard the screaming girls, saw the crowd, and came running blowing his whistle.

"Hey there, folks, let's disperse now!" he said. "Get away from the railing. We're going to have to get emergency vehicles in here." Already he was on his radio calling in to headquarters to send everything they had to Atlantic and 36th Streets by the old fishing pier right beside the Norwegian Lady Plaza.

"Come on, Jess, let's get out of here!" Nick grabbed her hand and started dragging her after him. "Do you want to get in trouble or something?"

"No, that girl's out there!" Jessie fought him

every step of the way. "Do you think I can just walk off?"

But Nick wouldn't stop this time. He took it upon himself to literally yank Jessie off the beach and carry her up the stairs. He obviously didn't care if she pounded his back with her fists when he threw her up over his shoulder. He hurried off down the boardwalk to where he had his car parked.

"Jessie! Nick! Wait!" It was Trish and Dot heading for them at a dead run from the direction of the shopping plaza next to the Big Surf Hotel. Their packages slapped against their jeans. You could spot Trish anywhere. She was six feet tall with curly black hair that spilled down over her shoulders.

"What's going on here, you two? I know it can't be Tarzan and Jane, but it does look odd with you slung over Nick's shoulder," said Trish, catching her breath and pushing her hair back from her face.

Nick put Jessie down.

If she'd been in a different mood Jessie would have laughed. Trish always looked so oddly put together. Her shoes didn't match, and her jeans were halfway up her calves. She was fun to have around and she usually made Jessie feel better no matter what was wrong.

But there was too much wrong now to feel anything but numb with shock.

Still Jessie was grateful that Trish was trying.

Trish's sixteen-year-old sister Dot was always in a hurry. She tapped Trish on the shoulder. "Trish, I think we'd better get going. Here comes the policeman." Dot was a thin little girl with a ponytail who was always afraid the worst was going to happen. She always seemed to be bouncing up and down on the balls of her feet because she couldn't stand still. But both of them had been Jessie's friends forever, and she knew they had her welfare in mind.

They all started toward the parking lot, but it was too late.

The shrill whistle froze everyone right in their tracks. "All right, kids! Halt! I saw you down on the beach." A harried-looking policeman caught up with them. He took off his hat and wiped the sweat from his brow.

Nick had been trying to avoid all this trouble. He shuffled his feet and stuck his hands deep into his pockets. He let Jessie do the talking.

"I saw everything." Jessie went forward, clasping her hands. "I was with the girl when she drowned." She didn't know what kind of trouble she was getting into, but she had to tell the truth.

Emergency vehicles were arriving. Another officer was waving to the cop talking to them. "I don't have time now. I'll question you all later," said the officer. "Stand right here until I get back."

"Thanks, Jess!" sighed Trish, as the officer hurried away. She rolled her eyes as they were herded over to a place by the railing where the reporters were beginning to set up their cameras and remotes. She leaned on the railing with one elbow, precariously balanced on one foot. "I always wanted to know what it was like to be arrested."

"Jess, what's going on?" whispered Dot as she looked nervously from side to side.

Nick shuffled along beside the girls. He didn't seem to want to make eye contact with anybody.

A female officer with short, cropped black hair arrived in a moment and started taking down all the facts and figures from Jessie. This officer wanted to know everything. Where had she first met the girl? What was her name? What did she look like? How old was she? Had they been friends for long? Had they ever quarreled? Her pencil point moved with the utmost precision across her tablet.

"Now wait a minute," interrupted Nick. "You don't mean to imply my friend Jessie was mixed up in anything, do you?"

"Jessie's never been mixed up in anything in her life," Dot almost pleaded. Tears were coming to her eyes.

"That's what we're trying to determine," said the policewoman with a cold, emotionless face.

Nick stood close to Jessie, trying to lend her his support by his hovering presence. He leaned back against the railing and said very quietly, "*This* was what I was trying to prevent, Jess." He answered the questions the policewoman put to him as plainly as possible. No, he hadn't seen the girl. He'd never met her before or known anyone who fit that description — about seventeen, female, tall, athletic-looking, and blond with blue eyes.

"I will answer any questions — any questions at all." Jessie gave Nick a nasty stare. "Anything that might help find her body and maybe put her on life support. We can always hope for a miracle. You ought to know that, Nick Stieveson. Your father's a surgeon."

By now the emergency vehicles were screeching up on the boardwalk. The ever-growing crowds of spectators were herded behind ropes by rows upon rows of police, who seemed to gather from every direction. Traffic on Atlantic Avenue was stopped by roadblocks to allow room for the larger ambulances and fire engines to park. People abandoned their cars just to see what was happening and surged forward, breaking down the barricades until the police threatened them with arrest.

An ambulance with its siren screeching and its red light flashing careened up to the boardwalk steps. A CPR unit leaped out of the truck with their equipment in hand and took the steps two at a time down to the beach. They laid out their stretchers and blankets near the water's edge.

The next police van zoomed up the boardwalk at such a pace the old wooden boards creaked and the ancient pier rattled. Men in wet suits jumped out. They put on their masks and fins, leaped over the boardwalk railing, and dove into the sea. Helicopters moved into view swooping down as low as they could to get a closer look. The coast guard cutters and police boats could be heard long before they reached the scene. They plowed through the water dragging nets and chains between them.

"Look at those hooks!" said Dot. "What do they use those for?"

"They have to dredge for the body," said Nick grimly but calmly.

Dot put her hand to her neck and hid her face against Jessie's shoulder. Jessie felt her friend sobbing and responded automatically. She stroked Dot's hair again and again and whispered words of comfort she couldn't even remember later. At least this friend felt warm — and alive. The girl on the surfboard had to be dead. No one could stay alive out there that long without breathing. Jessie swallowed hard.

The stranger had seemed so vital, more alive than anyone Jessie had ever met. Her facial expressions had been so lively and her smile winning. She had just exuded energy with her wild performances on the surfboard. And such spirit — to tempt fate so when a storm was coming on! Where had she gone? One moment she seemed on top of the world. Nothing could stop her. And the next . . .

Jessie bit her lip. It was almost as if she had known the girl. A sob wanted to come out, but

Jessie fought to keep it down even though it burned her throat. She had to be quiet for Dot's sake. Her friend was already upset enough — and Jessie supposed she was probably responsible for that, too.

Let's face it. She, Jessie, had let the girl die. That made her a murderer.

Jessie felt a strong hand on her shoulder. A special warmth radiated from that hand. Without turning around, she knew it must be Nick. He might be annoying most of the time, but in a situation like this she needed him.

She almost didn't hear the questions the newspaper and television reporters flung at her. It was almost as if she were a politician running for state or local office.

"Did she tell you ahead of time she was going to kill herself?" the KRRX-TV reporter said, holding the mike up to Jessie's mouth.

"I . . . ah . . ." Jessie wet her lips. Suddenly her throat went dry. Her voice wouldn't work.

"Can't you see she's been through enough? Why don't you leave her alone?" Nick stepped in front of Jessie. He stood there with his legs apart, glaring back at the crowd of journalists.

But a reporter shoved him aside. "Was it a

suicide pact? We hear so much about teen-agers trying to take their lives today. How does it feel to be a survivor?"

A *Virginia Times* reporter came very close to screaming in her ear, "What does it feel like to almost drown?"

The press of the crowd . . . the mob . . . the sea of faces . . . It was suffocating. Suddenly Jessie remembered her dream about the black seawater pressing down on her lungs, forcing all the air out of them. She had to get out of there. The police said they were finished with their questions — for now. There was nothing left to do.

"Nick?" Jessie looked around. He was right by her side. "You're right for once. Let's get out of here."

Nick took her hand.

"All right, everybody, you've had your victim for the day," Trish yelled to the reporters. "I'm sure you'll sell a lot of newspapers." She tried to clear a way through the crowd along with Dot. But it was Nick who led the way. Some of the reporters persisted in following them and shouting questions, but none of them paid any attention.

"Wait a minute!" The voice was coming from the beach.

"Hurry," said Nick, looking over his shoulder.

It was one of the scuba divers. "Is this yours?" He handed Jessie a necklace of seashells with a round crystal pendant. It was the necklace the girl was wearing when she went under. The turquoise in the center of the crystal seemed to glow.

Dot and Trish were puzzled. Jessie burst into tears and turned away. Nick gazed at it in horror.

"I told you she was real!" Jessie protested. She and her friends got into Nick's car and he slammed the car doors behind them. "This proves it." She held the necklace up to his face.

It was perfect, just like the girl who had worn it. Jessie held the solid gold chain strung with tiny, coral-colored shells. When she fingered them she could tell at once these were not cheap imitations — they were actual shells from the sea. Each one had slight imperfections on its surface, but each surface was lustrous and glowed and invited her fingers to roam over each shell and rest in tiny nooks and cavities.

In the center of the strand hung the jewellike

pendant, a beautiful crystal as fine as a diamond with a diamond's fire and brilliance. But most breathtakingly beautiful of all was the fine blue-green turquoise imbedded in the crystal's center. How had it gotten there without damaging the crystal?

"I'm glad you didn't tell the scuba diver the necklace wasn't yours." Trish sighed from the back seat of Nick's Saab. "They probably would have kept us for more questions. And I'm sure they are doing everything they can for this poor girl, whoever she was. We certainly can't do anything more."

Nick was taking the girls home now that the traffic was starting to break up. They'd decided to leave Jessie's Buick in the parking lot and come back for it later. Her friends didn't trust her to drive. The girl's body hadn't been found. The search was continuing, but hopes were also dying. Everybody wanted to get home and get on with their lives. The excitement was over.

"Yeah," added Dot, "you looked so pale and so shocked I thought you were going to faint."

"Why did you have to tell them it was my necklace? That's a lie!" Jessie insisted.

"Let's get away from here," said Nick, looking worried. "I'm sure you'll feel better, Jess, as soon as I get you home."

"That's easy for you to say," Jessie mumbled under her breath as she stuffed the necklace into her pocket. She crossed her arms defiantly and slumped down in her seat. "You don't have crazy parents like mine."

Jessie knew she wasn't being fair to Nick. He couldn't help it if he came from one of the richest families in Virginia Beach. Home for him was one of the few remaining beachfront houses on what was locally known as "The Strip." He lived close to the plushest hotels and fanciest restaurants in town. He could walk right out of his bedroom, down some stairs, and out onto the sand. His two sisters, who looked like miniature versions of their mother and nothing like Nick, lived there — and both his parents.

Nick's father was a well-known surgeon who worked at the Norfolk Memorial Hospital and had, early on, made a killing in real estate. He'd sold off old family properties inherited from some ancestral sea captain.

Nick's mother was a society lady. She always sported a tall, blond updo and fancy clothes. She didn't have to work but she joined all the local ladies' clubs, and was the only mother Jessie knew who was always there waiting when Nick came home from school.

Jessie flicked on the radio to keep herself from going crazy. She had left her Walkman at the beach and needed something to do with her fingers. She switched randomly from station to station, AM to FM, and back again. Madonna was on one station and Pearl Jam on another.

Nick stared at her grimly.

By chance, or so it seemed at first, she tuned in the news. It was six o'clock, and the local report was on. *"A drowning in the Atlantic off the coast of The Strip today. All this and more in a moment,"* said the newscaster as they broke away for a commercial.

Jessie couldn't move. She heard Dot and Trish suck in their breaths. Nick gripped the steering wheel tightly with both hands. As he neared Pacific Avenue, the traffic got heavy. It was rush hour, but Nick didn't seem to notice. He ran a red light. Horns honked, but Jessie just turned up the radio. She had to hear this.

"Local Virginia Beach High School junior Jessie Rogers was the only witness to a drowning around five o'clock this afternoon at the old pier near the Norwegian Lady Plaza. According to

her story, which the police are at this hour examining, an unknown, as yet unidentified, high school girl was seen surfing in the area where there have already been two drownings this spring. The missing girl was described as being about six feet tall with long blond hair and blue eyes. Police have been unable to recover her body. We do not know what the two girls were doing on the beach in this unauthorized area. The police have not disclosed whether they will charge the surviving girl with trespassing.

The beach has been closed to the public since April 1, when the drownings of two local high school boys occurred. There has been much talk about dismantling the old pier for safety reasons, but the Virginia Beach Historical Society has so far blocked all attempts. It claims that the pier is a National Historic Landmark because of its proximity to the Norwegian Lady Plaza and should be preserved and renovated . . ."

Nick flicked off the radio.

There was dead silence and then Jessie said, "Do you know how much trouble I'm in, guys? My mother listens to the news on her drive home. There's no way she won't know what happened!"

"Well, I always wanted to be famous," said Trish. "Now I'm not so sure."

"Don't think you're the only one, Jess," said Dot. "Our mom'll find out, too, and when she does we'll be grounded for a month — maybe even all summer if she gets mad enough."

Nick said nothing. He just slowed the car down after he left the Virginia Beach Expressway and headed for the tree-lined Great Neck Road. Towering oaks shaded his black Saab as it purred down the street. But just as Jessie had feared, her mother's old white Chrysler K car was pulling into the driveway ahead of them — *just* ahead of them. Her stomach did flip-flops.

Slowly Jessie opened the door of the Saab and got out, followed by her friends. They seemed to sense that Jessie needed their support. Nick was right behind her.

Things were even worse than she had feared. Her mother sprang out of the driver's seat with the swiftness of a wildcat when she saw Jessie in the rearview mirror. Her mother stood there in the driveway, tapping her foot. She was wearing one of her severe work suits — a black skirt, a black-and-white pinstriped jacket, and pointed black heels. She'd put on her stern, schoolmarm look that had frightened a generation of Virginia Beach High

School history students into instant submission.

Mrs. Rogers had very dark eyes and had a way of glaring that looked nothing short of ominous, especially when accentuated by her horn-rimmed glasses. "Jessie Rogers," she said in that tone of voice that brooked no nonsense, "get into that house right now."

"But — "

"I said right now, young lady!" Mrs. Rogers always made it a point never to raise her voice. She got her point across very well without it.

"Mrs. Rogers, I think I can explain." Nick stepped forward.

"Nick Stieveson, I'm shocked, to say the very least, that you're mixed up in this! A nice boy like you. What will your mother and father say?"

"But it didn't happen the way you think," Nick dared to say.

"I thought you were a boy we could trust. I thought you had some sense in your head and were a good influence on our Jessie. I don't expect you to encourage her worst tendencies."

Jessie sighed. Jessie's "worst tendencies" were her mother's sore spot — and her dad's, too. She had accused Jessie from the time she was a little girl of having "worst tendencies" and a penchant for getting into trouble. Her mind wandered at school. She didn't pay attention, and she always seemed to be the "bleeding heart" who got herself into trouble by meddling in other people's problems.

Jessie hung her head, speechless. But that was nothing compared to her shock when her father got out of her mother's car with the family lawyer.

"Dad!" Jessie gulped and took a step backward.

If her mother had a scary presence, Dad had ten times as much. He was the principal at the high school where his wife taught. He not only towered above everyone else, he had the brawn and shoulders to intimidate any of the school's troublemakers. Jessie had often seen him keep order all by himself. That was the reason Virginia Beach High had one of the lowest crime rates and best attendance records in the state. Now that towering presence was descending upon her.

"Jessie Rogers!" he stood toe-to-toe with her. "I rely upon you to set a good example for the rest of the school. What do you have to say for yourself?"

"Nothing," she said, hanging her head. There was no way she could make him understand. None of them seemed to understand. They all thought she was crazy — from Nick, to Trish and Dot, to her parents. Maybe she *was* nuts. She had imagined talking to a stranger on a surfboard. She had even thought she felt the half-drowned body in her arms before it was pulled away from her. But then, how could that have happened? How could the girl disappear without a trace?

"Dr. Rogers," Nick broke in, sounding as respectful as he could, "she just tried to save a girl she thought was drowning. She thought she saw somebody out there."

Why doesn't he say I ought to be locked in the loony bin? Jessie said to herself.

Trish and Dot were obviously shocked at Nick's nerve in standing up to the school principal.

Dr. Rogers inhaled sharply. "Nick, you know as well as I do that there was no good reason for either of you to be on that beach today. It was unsafe and had been closed down for a good reason. You were breaking the law. That's something young people have too little respect for. You could have gotten yourselves killed."

"Jessie almost did get herself killed," Dot's voice squeaked. "Nick saved *her* from drowning."

Mrs. Rogers paled. Dr. Rogers was speechless for a moment. The lawyer stood silently beside the car, tensely gripping the door handle.

"I know, Dad, I know. I'm going," Jessie finally said. She slipped past everyone into the house and locked herself in her bedroom. Only then did the shock of everything she had just gone through sink in.

Only then did she cry.

Chapter 3

After her friends had been sent home, Jessie listened from her room as her parents sat down at the dining room table with Mr. Evans. He was the family lawyer and her parents had known him forever. They were drawing up their child custody plans. Her parents were getting divorced.

"At seventeen, Jessie is at an age where the judge might ask her with whom she prefers to live," said Mr. Evans, bringing up a point that no one had considered.

"You would think she was old enough, but she certainly doesn't act it," said Mrs. Rogers. Her shrill voice penetrated Jessie's bedroom door, even though it was on the second floor.

"She obviously needs close parental supervision," said Dr. Rogers in his low, commanding voice. "At least we agree on that."

But the conversation soon degenerated into a battle, each parent blaming the other for Jessie's lapses of judgment. Mrs. Rogers accused her husband of not laying down the law. Dr. Rogers accused his wife of doing too little to help Jessie get over her "worst tendencies." Perhaps Mrs. Rogers wasn't stern enough. At any rate, his wife's relatives certainly seemed to be kooky enough — all a bunch of daydreamers and drifters.

"It all started when she was a kid. Remember that time she walked on the newly poured cement driveway and got her shoes stuck in the muck?" Dr. Rogers said. "We'd just bought them for her fourth birthday and had to throw them away."

"Yes," said Mrs. Rogers, "you were supposed to be watching her. But you were on the telephone talking to the superintendent!"

"She's always so impulsive," complained Dr. Rogers. "She just had to run out into the street to save that damn cat. The car swerved and hit a tree, and that cat bit her for all her pains."

"Again," Mrs. Rogers tapped her fingers smartly on the table, "you were supposed to be watching her while I was doing laundry. But you were gabbing to the neighbors."

"If you think it's all my fault, how about that time when she turned sixteen and got her driver's license. I was out of town at an education conference. Jessie just had to pick up that hitchhiker, and he stole the car while she was paying for gas at the service station."

Jessie lay on her bed, pulled the sheets over her head, and rolled over. When that didn't block out the sound of her parents' voices, she stuffed a pillow over her head. At last she fell asleep.

The last thing she remembered to do before she closed her eyes was to lay the pendant-and-shell necklace on the nightstand beside her bed. It was the least she could do for the unfortunate girl, keep her necklace. It looked valuable, and once her body was found and identified her relatives might come asking for it.

She was grounded indefinitely, and she knew it. It was the sort of thing her parents always did. They pretended to care about her, but it seemed that they were only interested in their endless battles with each other. She felt like an excuse.

It was a warm night, if a breezy one, with a nice saltwater scent in the air. Jessie had left her windows open to let the night air blow in on her. It relaxed her. Her mind was so numb with shock that she had almost forgotten her fear of falling asleep. But no sooner had she drifted off — or so it seemed — than she heard a voice. It whispered, *"Jessie."*

Jessie opened her eyes and shook herself. She looked around, barely conscious of what she was doing. Then, when she heard nothing else, she closed her eyes and drifted back off to sleep. She pulled the sheet over herself a new way. Her mind, exhausted from the day's events, told her it was just the wind. It was either the wind or the tree branches rustling against the roof.

This time she'd hardly had a chance to let her mind go blank when she heard the voice again, this time a much louder hiss, *"Jessie!"*

Jessie sat straight up in bed, her heart pounding, and the hair on the back of her neck standing on end. She waited alone in the dark, holding her breath to hear it again.

"Is someone here?" She swallowed hard when no reply came. Her heartbeat seemed to keep track of the seconds of silence.

"I don't think this is funny, whoever it is." She spoke out loud to give herself courage. She rose from bed and carefully made the rounds of her bedroom, looking for intruders.

The light would not go on. The high winds had probably caused the power to go out.

She checked in the closet. There was nothing but a rack thick with her dresses, tops, and jeans. She looked under her bed. Her hand touched only vacant space. Behind the door . . . there was nothing but the blank wall, still smelling faintly of the dousing of new paint her father had given it just before he'd moved out.

Everything was safe and familiar.

Maybe it was the radio. She suddenly remembered the old-fashioned clock radio on her dresser, the one her parents had given her. Her mother had used it in college. It was so old it didn't even have a digital face, but it still worked — after a fashion. She only used it on the mornings when she had to get up for school. It always had static. Perhaps she had bumped the "on" button in her sleep and it had come on during the night. That had to be what was "speaking" to her.

Jessie sat back down on her bed with new confidence and yanked the radio's plug out of the wall. She'd get rid of it in the morning. If she couldn't get a good night's sleep with this thing beside her bed, she'd just have to buy a new alarm clock.

"Jessie, why don't you listen to me? I need you."

A cold sweat broke out on her forehead. Now there could be no mistaking it. The voice was right beside her — and sounded very familiar. It was the same voice that had called her name. Suddenly Jessie felt the drowning girl's cold fingers against her neck and her cheeks as she tried to pull her to shore.

"Help me, Jessie! Help me!" The voice sounded pitiful, like a child crying.

"What do you want from me?" Jessie asked. "If you're a ghost — if you're dead — I can't help you now."

"Help!" The final cry sounded strangled, forced, as if someone was taking a last breath. Jessie had the eerie sensation of somebody going under the water for the final time.

Jessie put her arms out to brace herself. Her hand struck the nightstand and landed on the shell necklace. It was warm and vibrating slightly. She cautiously put the necklace to her ear and listened to the sound of the sea inside one of the shells. But faintly, as if in the far distance, she could still hear the word, *"Help!"*

Jessie quickly dropped the necklace. What was going on? Maybe she was dreaming and this was all a nightmare. But Jessie knew she was too awake to be dreaming. Why *had* the scuba diver given her the necklace?

Jessie sat bolt upright and trembled with fear until she began to drowse off. But she didn't sleep for long before she felt the now-familiar suffocating sensation in her chest. It felt as if a great black weight were pressing down on her lungs, and this time she woke up gasping for breath.

Jessie knew what she had to do. This "thing" would not leave her alone. She hurried into her clothes. She was past caring what her mother would say as she eased her way down the stairs in the dark. At least she was able to find her car keys easily enough. Her mother had confiscated them and hidden them in a kitchen drawer. Her father had taken a cab to the Norwegian Lady Plaza parking lot and driven her old, beat-up Buick home himself. He told her he would have it junked if he saw her driving it at any time during the next month.

The trouble she'd be in when her mother or father found out what she was about to do was the farthest thought from her mind. She didn't feel she had a choice. She silently hurried out the front door and headed for her car. She got in, closed the car door as quietly as possible, started the motor, and made her way down Great Neck Road. Towering oaks, which lined both sides of the street, seemed to sigh above her. As the wind blew their branches wildly about, they began to remind Jessie of the wavy green depths. They seemed to lead the way.

Jessie knew she had to find the body. It might have washed up on the beach. Maybe the girl's spirit couldn't rest. She wanted to have it buried properly before the seagulls and dogs got to it. Maybe then she could put this whole matter to rest. Her parents would certainly be happy with that.

Jessie's plan wasn't going to be as easy as she had hoped. Even in the wee hours of the morning the streets of Virginia Beach were heavily traveled. She'd had the expressway pretty much to herself, but there were always revelers on the waterfront. Roadblocks and police barricades had been erected all around the Norwegian Lady Plaza. Even the nearby parking lot was closed off to all traffic. There were signs everywhere: NO TRESPASSING. VIOLATORS WILL BE PROSECUTED.

"Oh, boy!" she sighed. "More trouble. Here we go again."

There were no available parking spaces on

the same side as the beach, even at that hour, so Jessie left the car in the lot, which was across the street, and walked back to the Norwegian Lady Plaza. She tried to keep an easy pace so no one would get suspicious.

Jessie had never believed in ghosts. Now she didn't know what to believe. If someone asked her in school she would still have to say, "No way," or, "You watch too much TV."

Yet she was beginning to wonder who was trying to communicate with her and for what purpose. She was only human. She could do very little. If there were ghosts, they were immortal. What could she do that they couldn't? Everything was very confused and very mixed up. But there was one thing she was sure of — she wasn't crazy and she wasn't imagining things. This was real.

She sneaked around the Big Surf Hotel without a policeman or a passerby spotting her. Soon she was on the boardwalk. She lost her self-consciousness as she walked over to the railing and gazed out to sea.

The moon was full tonight. An eerie silver glow illuminated the cresting waves as they came crashing against the shore. Each wave caused the planking of the boardwalk itself to creak and groan in protest. The wind was still up, and it threw her hair back away from her face at one moment and then whipped it around her neck the next. The foam and salt spattered her face and clothes.

She scanned the beach — or what used to be the beach — beneath her. The tide was running so high tonight it had lapped it up and coiled around the posts driven into the sand that supported the boardwalk structure.

The body could not be here. There was no place for it to rest.

She had to get closer. Closer to *what* she was not sure. Jessie simply could not see from where she stood. She headed for the old pier. The beach approach had been cut off by the sea, and the pier was hard to reach from the new boardwalk. A narrow walkway had been created to connect the two, and she knew the way.

Jessie had to climb over a lot of barricades and cross over a rickety stretch of planking to reach it. But then, just as she was about to run out to the end, she was stopped dead in her tracks. It was so dark out there, and despite the bright moonlight that illuminated the sea, the old pier was shrouded with a blackness so thick that she almost couldn't breathe. It was suffocating.

Jessie was suddenly struck with a wave of panic so strong that she could hardly stand straight on her own two feet. There was someone — or something — out there waiting for her. She could feel it — icy fingers reaching out to touch her and creeping down her neck . . . cold sweat.

The pier started to shake. It wasn't just the force of the waves striking the old wood. There was something coming toward her. She distinctly heard footsteps. She couldn't move. Her feet were rooted to the spot. Her heart was pounding. It was almost as if she could hear the words, *"Jessie, help me!"*

Jessie couldn't bear to see that pale white face and the silvery blond hair of the corpse, now dead all these hours. She thought of hair intertwined with seaweed.

A hand cupped itself over her mouth and smothered her screams, which came one right after the other. They were forced back down into her throat by the pressure of the strong, relentless fingers.

"Jessie, Jessie, it's me!" came the voice. But it was not low and whispery. It was a voice she had known for years. It was Nick.

She groaned, turned, and threw her arms around him. He held her tightly for a moment, and their hearts beat together so rapidly that Jessie could not tell hers from his. He might be meddling, but she had never been so glad to see him. She was saved. She was not going to die. She was not going to touch anything already dead. Nick was warmer than she was. She was so cold — and he was so close. For a moment it seemed she could forget everything but her head resting against his chest.

Finally she said, "What are you doing here?"

He paused. "I knew you'd be here."

"Nick, nobody made you my keeper. You heard what my parents said. Do you want to get in trouble?"

"Yeah, Jess, do you think I care when your life is at stake?" He put his finger under her chin and tilted her head. The moon backlit his body, and she could barely make his face out of the shadows. "This pier is crumbling even as we stand on it. That's why it's closed down. Even the pilings on the boardwalk have been damaged by the storm. And I knew you'd come here and try to do some crazy, lunatic thing."

They had seemed so close for an instant, but now Jessie could see Nick's silly arrogance — thinking he was better, more sane, more stable, more responsible than she was — was rearing its ugly head once again.

"OK, Nick." She pushed herself away. "Time for you to check out. I have to do what I have to do, and I don't need you here."

She turned away from him and headed out toward the end of the old pier. As she'd expected, he followed her and grabbed her arm, but this time she was ready for him. "All right, 'Mr. Do-Gooder,' now what are you going to do? Carry me off the beach again? Where will you take me? To the police? You're all ready in hot water with them just like me. To my parents? They'd probably call the police, they're so angry. Then just think of the look on *your* parents' faces when their sweet, adorable, perfect little boy gets into trouble!"

Jessie defiantly sat herself down on the edge of the pier and dangled her legs as she always did. She didn't think Nick would stay with her after that. Perhaps she'd been too cruel to him, but . . .

"All right, Jess, you win." Nick finally sat himself down beside her after a long pause. "Do you know why I really came here tonight?"

"I just couldn't guess," she said sarcastically.

She waited a long while for his answer.

"I lied to you." His voice sounded odd,

strained. "I saw the girl on the surfboard, too, this afternoon. I just didn't want to admit it."

At first Jessie didn't think she'd heard right. Then the meaning of his words sank in — slowly. A wave of incredible relief washed over her. She *wasn't* crazy. She couldn't be. This was her absolute proof. It had all really happened, every last event of that crazy, mixed-up day.

"Nick, why didn't you tell me before? Why did you tell everyone I was imagining the girl, that I was just talking to myself?" She put her hand on his arm.

When no answer was forthcoming — none of his usual excuses — she knew there was something strange going on. He didn't say, "Oh, gee, Jess, I didn't want them to think I was a loony, too." Or, "What would my father say?" or even, "If the police thought a guy was involved in the drowning, too, they'd be much more likely to suspect foul play."

Instead he just remained silent, staring off into the star-filled sky. The waves broke against the pier and sent salt spray up to mist their faces and fleck their hair with spume.

"Nick, why don't you answer me?" she finally repeated, shaking his arm.

Still he did not reply. He would not even turn toward her.

"Nick, tell me why else you came here tonight!" She shook him. "Did — did you hear a voice? Did someone call you?" A ghastly intuition popped into her head. Shivers went up her spine as she remembered the voice — that low, whispery sound of someone in pain.

Her hair was standing on end. She expected him to say, "Yes," but instead he placed his hand over hers. Jessie did not take hers away.

"Jessie, before I answer you, will you let me tell you something?"

"Yes, of course," she said. Suddenly she remembered how strange Nick had been acting that day — not at all himself.

He had been nervous and brooding the whole time. Normally he was strong and self-confident. He had still taken on the police as well as her father — risking everybody's wrath. He had still acted like "Mr. Good Guy" saving her life. But he had acted with a sort of desperate energy as if, well, yes, as if something were pursuing him — as if Nick saw something that even she did not.

"Jessie . . ." he began. "I know we haven't always gotten along . . ."

"That's all right, Nick. Not now."

"But you've really got to believe some-thing . . ."

"Yes?"

Jessie saw him wet his lips before going on. "I did everything I did today, Jess, because I had to. I did it for you. You see, I've always kind of liked you, I guess. Can you believe that?"

His hand was still covering hers. "Yes," she said. A flush was creeping up her neck, but she also felt a warmth in her own heart. He'd always been able to hurt her more than any-body else — except her parents. But that was because they had always been so close.

He turned toward her suddenly. He put his arm around her waist and pulled her near. They were so close now she could feel his warm breath on her cheek. She sensed the nearness of his lips before they brushed hers ever so gently. Then they returned with a full kiss. Slowly her arms went around his neck.

He kissed her again and again, but then he suddenly stood up, pulling her to her feet after him. "You've got to come with me, Jess. I must show you something."

Chapter 4

Jessie had never seen Nick's house at 4:00 A.M., but she thought it was strange that all of the lights seemed to be on.

"Are your parents having a party?" Jessie asked even though she didn't see any cars.

"No, they're not home."

Jessie knew her parents would probably freak if they knew she was at Nick's when his parents were not there. But Nick was not just any guy. She'd known him for years, and yes — despite their differences — she trusted him. And of course the eerie experience of the day and night negated everything else.

"They're on a Bermuda cruise. They've taken my sisters with them. Some sort of surgeons' convention. Otherwise I probably wouldn't have been allowed out of the house after what's happened today."

"Why all the lights?"

"An old mariner's tradition," he said. "The house is right on the water, you know." He sounded very serious. "Ships lost at sea or foundering in a storm and all. They expect a light on land to guide their way."

"I never thought of that."

"If you've been here once, you've been here a thousand times." Nick led the way into the front hallway. Nick's house always made her say, "Wow!" Everything was ultramodern — what people called "the Scandinavian look," with light woods and polished teak, metal, glass, and thick black leather everywhere. As he led her up the stairs, Jessie noticed how Mrs. Stieveson had collected even more priceless crystal vases and all sorts of expensive bric-a-brac since the last time they had been here together. When Dr. Stieveson went convention-hopping, his wife went shopping.

"But, Nick, what does your secret have to do with what's been happening to us — this girl and all?" Jessie asked as they reached the landing.

Nick opened a locked doorway that led to a third floor. She'd never known there was one. Jessie thought the highest-placed windows in the house were just an attic. But instead, there was a large, airy room furnished with antiques from the last century. All sorts of maps and charts, paintings of ships, and oils of people in old-fashioned dress hung on the walls. The walls were covered with bookshelves filled with dusty ancient tomes on sea lore.

"What's this?" She walked up to a telescope-like contraption in front of the spacious bay windows. The windows opened onto a veranda, or rather onto a narrow, porchlike balcony.

"That's called a spyglass and that beyond is a widow's walk," Nick said. "The spyglass was used to spot ships at sea. The captain's wife used to pace back and forth on the widow's walk to see if her husband was returning home. All too often he didn't come back."

"So everybody in your family's lived here — since the beginning?"

"Since the first Captain Stieveson came here from Norway in the eighteen nineties."

"And they were all sea captains?"

"Just the first."

Somehow Nick was making everything he said sound rather ominous. "But what does this have to do with me?" she asked.

The moonlight was pale on Nick's face, but he managed to look even paler. His green eyes were usually lively, but now seemed far away and rather wan. Nor was there much expression on his face. "Why don't you just sit right there, Jessie, and let me tell you." Nick pointed out a big, old, leather-covered chair that smelled of cigar smoke and, ever so faintly, of the sea itself. It was a very masculine smell, and Jessie could imagine a sea captain owning it.

"Nick, are you all right?" Jessie said. All he seemed capable of was staring into space. Then, suddenly, he began to speak. His story was a long one.

At the end of the last century, Captain Olaf Stieveson was a happy man. Or at least so he fancied himself. He owned the swiftest ship on the seas, *The Norwegian Lady,* ran a small shipping company in Norway, and enjoyed robust health. He always loved a sea voyage and a brisk wind blowing in his face.

One day he even had the fortune to fall in love.

Ingrid was a woman of fantastic beauty. She appeared to come from a landed family that owned a castle by the sea. In fact, the captain had first seen her walking on the shore and had fallen in love with her long before they were formally introduced. She was tall with beautiful blond hair that looked just like flax from the loom. Her skin was so fair it was like the white clouds of summer. Her color was never high. That showed, so he thought, how delicate she was. And her eyes were such a pale blue they looked like pools of standing water in which one could see reflected the sky overhead.

She would stroll on the rocky coast and mesmerize him with her grace. It seemed that even the birds paid homage to her. They landed on her shoulders and on the top of her head. She talked to them, cooed, and spoke their language. Long before she and Olaf ever exchanged words, she used to wave at him as the captain sailed past the coast. He would lean way over the rail and wave back.

It got so that he would look for the girl as soon as he neared the coast. One day, during foul weather, he was turning his eyes toward the shore when he gave the wrong order. He could not keep his attention on the navigation and turned the ship into a wind that was blowing at nearly full-gale strength. His ship went down, and many of the crew were drowned. Even as the captain was sucked into the water he was thinking of those incredibly beautiful, vivid-blue eyes that he would now never get a chance to meet face-to-face.

The captain's body washed up on shore, clinging to a piece of driftwood. The girl with the tresses the color of flax found him on the beach and had her servants bring him home with her. The servants despaired for his life, but they also knew of their mistress's special powers. She checked him over minutely, putting a feather to his nostrils, and said, "His life force ebbs very low."

"Will you save him, lady?" asked her servant.

"He is very handsome. But that is up to him. It should be a pity if I have to let him die."

The girl lit a fire to keep him warm and began to mix her potions. She crushed berries, roots, and special spices together with her mortar and pestle and then mixed them into her cauldron. She raised his head just enough to wet his lips and then threw the rest of the brew into the flames. The flames leaped high on the hearth, and she waited until she could part the red from the white and that from the blue. It was to the blue she looked, as that was the hottest part of the flame.

"Well, Captain Olaf Stieveson, it is I who

call you as I have called you many times before. The Lady Ingrid is speaking. Can you hear me?"

"I am here," came the voice from the flames. It was the captain's.

"If I give you your life back, will you consent to be bound to me for the rest of your earthly days? I have your life here, in the palm of my hand."

There was silence. So the Lady Ingrid shooed her servants away, locked the door, and knelt down beside the fire. She took out one of her eyes. It was a bright crystal orb with the color blue tinting the surface. Embedded within it, right where her iris should be, was a light blue stone — like turquoise. Lady Ingrid set the eye down in front of the flames and commanded the captain, "Look into my eye. You will see all that you may have in life if you will only consent to be mine."

The eye clouded up, swirling with white mist. It showed a scene of sunlit waves and a prosperous fleet of ships all under the same flag. "You will become rich beyond measure," she said. "You will be commander of a great trading fleet, and you will reap their profits."

"Yes," said the captain's voice. "I have always wanted that."

The clouds then swirled back for a second, obscuring the view. When the scene became clear again, the young Captain Stieveson could be seen walking about in a crowd of old folks with canes. His back was not yet bowed. His step was as sprightly as ever. And she said, "You shall never grow old if you stay by my side."

"I have dreamed about that," said the captain's voice.

"And last of all you shall have me," she said. When the clouds cleared again, the captain could see Lady Ingrid herself walking by the shore. She looked up at him and seemed to smile and beckon. Her smile was bewitching. Her eyes held promise. And they were as clear and blue, as luminescent, as anything he could imagine. Her sweet scent seemed to drift out to him on the sea breezes and curl itself around his heart. He kept hearing her voice, "Come, my love, why don't you? Just say 'yes' and let yourself fly to me."

Her stare would not let him go. He peered into the eye and could not tear himself away. With its enchanting colors and proportions, with its promises, it mesmerized him. It grew brighter and brighter until it nearly blinded him.

"Yes," he said all in a rush. "Yes, yes, I agree."

"Very well, then, you shall live." The Lady Ingrid put her eye back and doused the flames. She performed her rituals on the body of the captain, and he slowly came back to life. All he remembered was waking up and staring up into the face of the lady he'd watched countless times on the shore. He felt as if he must remember her from some other place as well, for he felt as if he'd known her, known her well. Her smile now seemed familiar to him. And those turquoise eyes, that gaze, they frightened him a little but at the same time they kept him from turning away.

But during the first weeks of his convalescence, the captain hardly noticed anything but Lady Ingrid's beauty. He lay in bed in the castle and she brought him trays of food to tempt his appetite and broths to soothe and take away the chills of the North Sea, which lingered in his bones whenever he was out of her presence. He wanted, from time to time, to search the shore for the wreckage of his ship, *The Norwegian Lady,* and to bury the bodies of his crew that had washed up on the beach. But she quieted him and told him everything had already been taken care of. Her servants had buried the bodies and the ship was now in dry dock being repaired. Soon *The Norwegian Lady* would be better than new.

It was hard to remember anything else, let alone who he was, in the enchanting lady's presence. When he was better, he walked along the shore beside her and helped her gather shells. Each sounded like the sea. He was lulled into a dreamlike state. In fact, he wasn't quite sure if this wasn't all a dream. He feared he would wake up on *The Norwegian Lady* far out at sea.

None of the servants in the castle would answer any of his questions. He knew nothing about the lady who saved his life except that she was called Ingrid. Nor could he explain the lack of any other people on this coast. She did not seem to have any family and did not seem to care.

The lack of humans was more than made up for by the great numbers of animals. He had no idea that there was so much game, not to mention the pens of pigs, ducks, cows, and sheep that Lady Ingrid kept everywhere. In fact, the animals seemed to be very friendly, following Lady Ingrid about as he did. Their sad, soulful eyes did not escape him. At times he almost imagined that they were trying to speak to him, but of course that was insane. Everyone knew that animals could not talk.

He did think it peculiar when a seagull dove between Ingrid and him as they were walking on the beach one day holding hands. The bird flapped its wings in Lady Ingrid's face and squawked at the top of its lungs. She called upon one of her servants to shoot it. "You never can be too careful, you know," she smiled at Captain Stieveson as the bird fell to the ground. "Birds can carry dangerous diseases."

The whole incident chilled Olaf to the bone. "Did you really have to kill him? The bird meant no harm," the captain protested.

"He was my bird. I let him live here. He was ungrateful." She frowned for the first time since he had met her. "I don't like ungrateful creatures."

"But he — he was just a bird!" Olaf said.

Lady Ingrid remembered herself. Her returning smiles drowned out his fears for the time being. He just forgot about them as if they had never been.

Once he was fully recovered, the captain married Lady Ingrid. She insisted upon holding the ceremony aboard *The Norwegian Lady* and returning to his home with him. She said she had no regrets about leaving her coastline for a time and seeing the world in the company of her "dear captain." She smiled as she said the words and ogled him with those bright turquoise eyes of hers, upon which he could never turn his back and from which he could never look away. She looped her arm through his and walked forever at his side.

The captain later remembered the period of his greatest prosperity as starting with his marriage to Ingrid. From the moment he sailed away from her coastline in *The Norwegian Lady* he experienced nothing but one piece of luck after another. He built up a large fleet of trading ships and started an import–export company. Soon all the other Norwegian captains and seamen were working for him. His ships never sank, and they always encountered good weather. They reached port first and got the highest prices for their goods.

Ingrid was like a queen. While he was away she reigned supreme in his home port. She held great dinners and invited everyone who was anyone, including the nobility. People talked far and wide of the sumptuous dishes she served, including roast suckling pig and great sides of beef. Her overly elegant dinner presentations always seemed novel, and she urged everyone to eat a little more. No one could have noticed that the pigs with apples in their mouths and grapes for eyes appeared to have the same sad expressions as the animals on her estate. When asked where she got such delicious food, she said, "I import all my food from home, you know. I still keep a farm there."

The couple was blissfully happy. When she gave him a daughter, Olaf thought he was fit to burst at the seams with joy. When he asked questions, she reassured him everything was all right. "Are you sure you don't mind me leaving you alone so much?" he asked. His voyages were long, often of a duration of many months at a time. He counted every week and every day he spent away from her.

"No, my love, I keep myself amused," she said, pinching his cheek.

"I won't stay away from you for as long the next time."

"But you must if you are to be the greatest captain in all of Norway."

His friends started to whisper and tell stories about her. They gossiped about why she was so anxious to have her husband away at sea. She gave Olaf's friends orders to be at her beck and call, to appear at parties, and to follow her about as an entourage. Those who had dared to disobey her — and they were few because she was so frightening when crossed — had disappeared from town altogether. The whispers rumored they would never be seen by anyone again.

The gossip outraged Olaf. At first he challenged many men to pistol fights and socked a few more in the jaw, for he was above all a seaman. Finally his friends complained to him, "That wife of yours has you wrapped around her little finger. You'll believe anything she tells you."

"Yes, she has you bewitched," said another.

"You used to spend time going to the bars with us. Now you don't dine with anybody but that woman," said a third.

Olaf simply thought they were jealous of his happiness, and, by rights, they should be. He was no doubt the happiest man in the world.

One day he returned from a voyage earlier than anyone expected. He had rushed back just to see Ingrid. But she was nowhere to be found. Usually she made a point of meeting him at the docks. Or at the very least she would be standing at the top of the stairs and would make a graceful sweep down the staircase swishing her full skirts along in two hands. Then she would throw her arms around his neck and kiss him full on the lips. His little girl would also be waiting for him.

Today he listened expectantly for the light trip of Ingrid's step. But she was not in the house. The servants would not breathe a word about their mistress's whereabouts even when questioned. So he searched for his wife himself. He did not call out. He wanted to surprise her. From the second story bedroom he spotted her in the backyard arbor below, lecturing a servant who was on his knees crying.

He was about to call, "Ingrid!" when he caught sight of the ugly look on her face. She was staring at the wretched servant with the full force of those blue eyes, and the poor man would not defend himself anymore. She reached out and grabbed the servant by the neck. Would she strangle the poor man before Olaf's very eyes?

But as Olaf watched, the most incredible thing happened. The servant's yells changed from those of a man to the high-pitched squeals of a pig. In a minute Lady Ingrid was gripping a pig by the neck, nearly throttling it. She gave it a boot, and it ran off squealing.

The captain's blood ran cold. It was his misfortune that at that very moment she looked up and saw him. He had to pretend to smile. He came down to greet her, and she ran into his arms as always. But there was a difference. It was not as always and never could be again. He knew. She knew that he knew. And he knew that she knew it.

They did not speak of the change, but it haunted the captain. All his happiness turned to ashes. Too many events were now explained. Too many loose ends were tied up. He had always marveled at his fortune at surviving the shipwreck. He had wondered why none of his crew had lived. Now he had more than suspicions. He remembered the expressions of the animals on Ingrid's estate with a new poignancy. He swallowed hard.

He had to escape her despite his daughter. But Ingrid watched his comings and goings even more closely. She was now ever at his side. She was always smiling. But when she put her arm through his, she held on so tightly her fingernails made marks on his skin.

He could have no peace in Norway. He took to his ship and the sea. He stayed away longer and longer each voyage instead of rushing home as had been his custom. But as a cruel irony he prospered so much that he hardly had any reason to stay away. He had to return to Ingrid.

He opened up a trade route to the east coast of the United States. Of course this prospered instantly just like his other ventures, so fast that he began to suspect it was a spell. But at least it was far from Norway and even the shortest voyage kept him gone for months.

He docked in many American ports, primarily Boston, Philadelphia, and Savannah. But his favorite was Norfolk, and he loved the land around Virginia Beach. Any farther north and the beaches were too crowded. Any farther south and the weather became too unbearably muggy for one raised in Scandinavia.

So he built a house right there at Virginia Beach next to the port of Norfolk. He decorated it with bric-a-brac from his travels that sometimes took him as far afield as South America.

He found excuses to spend increasing amounts of time at his beach hideaway. During one visit he met a young girl by the name of Anna, whose father was a fisherman. Since he could not marry her, he made her his mistress. She made her home in their beach bungalow at Virginia Beach. It was Anna who paced the widow's walk, used the spyglass, and waited anxiously for her man to come home from the sea.

Anna was a gentle, simple lass and did not ask too much of her man except that he love her. She did not even complain when she bore him a son without a wedding band around her finger. She just named him "Olaf" after his father and adopted the captain's surname, "Stieveson."

After her son's birth Anna had to wait a long time for her captain to return. For upon his return to Norway, Ingrid told her husband, "You've achieved your life's desire. You're the richest captain in Norway, and I'm your wife. You don't need to go on any more voyages."

He could think of nothing to say. He knew her well. She wasn't making a request. She was laying down the law. But if he did not escape, he knew it would be his death. He remembered the squealing servant turned into a pig.

So he pretended to agree with her as he laid his plans in secret. He sent her to look for a house in the country as a retirement residence. She went, taking their daughter, without giving any indications of her suspicions when he said he would join her in a few days. He had only a few operations to close down and had to complete the sale of his shipping firm. "Then we can be together all the time," he said.

"Forever," she whispered in his ear as she kissed him good-bye.

As soon as he'd seen her carriage disappear down the street, he ran into the house. Captain Stieveson packed some clothes and a few belongings, and then he bolted for a waiting carriage. He ordered it to take him to the dock where *The Norwegian Lady* was waiting for him.

He had told the crew to remain aboard the ship on full alert, and they were now ready to cast off. The captain was the last man aboard. He already had informed the crew that they would have to find their own way back to Norway if they wished to return. *The Norwegian Lady* would never leave Norfolk again.

He would remember his Norwegian daughter in his will. He could not steal her away. Better she should remain in Norway than lead Ingrid to his door.

At first the captain was nervous that Ingrid would play one of her tricks. He began to relax only after they had left Norway behind and sailed for more southerly waters. She might be strange, she might have strange powers, but surely she would never be able to find him now. He had been very careful not to tell her he had a house at Virginia Beach. She knew about his American trade, but she would have to scour the coastline from Maine to Florida and then down to Rio de Janeiro as well to find him. His house was not easy to spot. It was concealed by sand dunes.

But as an extra precaution, they were not going to stay there. He had written Anna ahead of time to make sure she understood. She was to be waiting with her bag packed and the baby ready to leave. She was a fisherman's daughter and could be trusted with a boat. He would come as close to shore as he dared and flash a lantern for her. She would embark in her father's fishing boat, or a rowboat, and come aboard. Together they would sail to the Dismal Swamp of North Carolina, run the ship aground, and hide it there. They would disembark, move inland, and purchase a small farm where they could live in peace and quiet and be happy for the rest of their days.

As *The Norwegian Lady* neared Virginia Beach he was at the ship's rail morning, noon, and night. He even slept on deck with no company but that of the ship's gray tiger cat. Old Monk often sat on his shoulder and peered out to sea as eagerly as the captain did. The animal seemed to be equally anxious to land. "You want to escape, too, don't you?" he asked the cat.

The cat answered with a meow. It jumped down and rubbed against the captain's legs.

"When we get to North Carolina, you can come with us," he promised, and petted the cat's head. The cat merely stared at him with its big, luminous eyes.

They were very near Virginia Beach now. The captain could even see Anna's house. But the wind was picking up and was quite brisk. He did not want to be seen trying to pull closer to shore and yet he was impatient to get going. He did not want to waste any more time. Certainly a little wind was not going to bother one who had spent his whole life as a mariner.

Just as he was reaching for the lantern to signal Anna, he felt a claw on his skin. "Shoo, cat!" He tried to shove the animal away, but the cat clung to him, digging its nails into his arm. He attempted to shake himself free, not comprehending why the cat was yowling at the top of its lungs and trying to drive its long, piercing teeth into him. Angered, he finally struck the crazed animal with the lantern.

There on the deck beside him stood Ingrid,

glaring at him with her own luminous eyes. This time there was no pretense between them. "So, you thought to escape me, did you? And all for a girl named Anna!"

There was no use denying the truth. "Ingrid, let me go! You know there's nothing between us anymore."

"What can this Anna be to you after all that we have lived through together — after all that we have dreamed, built, and planned!" She advanced upon him like a cat stalking its prey.

She grabbed for the lantern, but Olaf kept it from her. She smiled at him evilly, the ends of her lips curling upward. "Very well, have it your own way, *my love!*" She said the last two words with a sneer.

Ingrid turned toward the railing and gazed out to sea. Even as she did so, the wind picked up again until it was almost gale strength. The ship tossed and turned, was hurled up from the waves and nearly swamped with seawater. As Olaf watched in horror, she removed her eye and held it before her. It glowed through the darkness of the night and made a beacon that could be seen all the way to the shore.

Olaf saw what she was trying to do and in

despair hurled himself at her. But he was too late, for on the beach Anna had been faithfully waiting. She had not brought her baby son with her. He had a bad cold, and his grandmother was minding him until Anna should become established in her new home. Anna did not think a sea voyage was just the thing for Little Olaf Stieveson right now.

But as soon as she saw the beacon, she did not despair of the foul weather. She was after all a mariner's daughter, and *The Norwegian Lady* could not be far offshore. Anna climbed into her boat and rowed ever outward toward the waiting ship tossing upon the waves. She never reached it. The sea rose in giant waves. Her boat was swamped, and she went down in sight of *The Norwegian Lady*, thinking of her lost love and of her child of love.

All was clearly visible to Olaf where he stood beside Lady Ingrid. "You fiend!" he said. "Who are you, anyway? What right do you have to destroy people's lives and make them subject to you?"

"You gave me yourself for saving your life. Remember?"

Even now in his misery, as the sea tossed about him, Olaf remembered. It was a kind of nightmare with her face hovering above him. There was a leaping flame, and he had promised himself to her.

"No." He shook his head. "Release me from my bond. I want to be free."

"You sold your soul to me for a passel of riches."

"Take the riches. Only give me back my Anna and my son," the captain wept.

"You shall never be free." She held out her eye toward him. As he backed away shaking his head, the crystal eye emitted a weird white light. It irradiated him in its milky sheen and he began to shrivel.

Olaf knew he was dying. He felt his very heart bursting within. But he was determined that the witch should not survive him. He called to his crew with his last breath to scuttle the ship and abandon it.

His next cries were of agony as he shrank from a full-size man to a tiny, hairless creature no bigger than a thumbnail in height, a dead-looking thing with yellow skin and no teeth. Lady Ingrid scooped him up and placed him in the center of the crystal eye, inside a turquoise prison in the blue heart of it. There would be nothing left of him but a voice, a faint, whispery voice, a voice that could only cry out for help even though there was no one powerful enough to help him — except Lady Ingrid.

As she was sucked down with the ship into the black ocean she uttered a curse. "You, Olaf, shall serve me. Your body is dead and gone, but your soul shall live forever. You and all the descendants that come from your bastard brat's line shall serve me. They are bound to the bond you made with me. You have given them into my care and my keeping. They are mine! They are all mine."

As the waves closed over her head, none of the seamen who survived the wreck knew whether Lady Ingrid had died. For when the storm cleared the next morning, there was no sign of her.

In that same year, 1897, the people of Norway remembered Captain Olaf Stieveson. They erected the bronze statue at Virginia Beach and called it "The Norwegian Lady."

"No one knew what happened to her — until now," Nick finished his tale. "Now I think she not only survived, but she's after you, Jessie."

Jessie sat still for a long time listening to the horrible tale. She did not remind Nick about the crystal jewel with the "blue eye," which had spoken to her. But she did not need to. He had seen it when the scuba diver gave it to her. Only now did she fully understand the horror on his face at that moment.

"Why should she be after me?" she asked. "I'm not a descendant of Captain Stieveson."

"I — I don't know," said Nick. "It's hard to understand this occult stuff. That's why it's better to leave it alone."

Jessie thought a long while. "Well, it seems 'this occult stuff' won't leave us alone, so we've got to find out."

"No!" Nick rested his hands on her shoulders and gently pushed her back into the old leather chair. "You've got to leave this mysterious power alone."

Jessie had something of her own to explain. "This force will kill me if I don't listen," she confessed. Up until now, she'd only told him of the whispery plea for help in the night. That's what brought her to the beach. What she hadn't told him about was her recurring nightmare. She described for Nick the suffocating sensation of having something black and heavy pressing on her lungs. It would not let her sleep, and without sleep she would surely die — or go crazy.

All the life drained from Nick's face. Then all the color flooded back in a rush as he exploded in anger. "Stay here with me. I'll protect you. I promise. I won't let anything happen to you."

Jessie knew that was impossible. Still, she didn't mind being enfolded in Nick's arms again. She was really too tired to resist and let herself be led to a sleeper sofa downstairs in the living room. There she bunked down for what remained of the night while Nick trudged wearily up to bed.

The next morning they were awakened by the sound of a car pulling into the driveway, footsteps coming up to the front door, and a key turning in the lock. Jessie staggered to the door and Nick came sleepily down the stairs just in time to see his parents walk into the living room.

"Why, Jessie, my, it's early to be visiting!" Nick's mother kissed her on the cheeks and then embraced Nick. "I'm glad you're here anyway. There's somebody I would like you both to meet."

Nick's sisters came through the door, carrying shopping bags. They had a new friend with them.

"Nick, Jessie, this is Marina Jacobsen. We met her on the cruise ship on the way back from Bermuda."

Jessie nearly fainted as Nick, aghast himself, moved swiftly to her side. It was the girl, the girl on the surfboard that everyone had been searching for yesterday. There was no mistaking it. The same long blond hair, the tall, graceful stance, the winning but mysterious smile, and the pale blue eyes that seemed to glow with a light all their own.

Chapter 5

"Trish . . . Trish, is that you?" Jessie said excitedly into the receiver of the phone. She paced back and forth with an electric sort of excitement. She couldn't have stood still if her life had depended upon it.

"Jess?"

"Trish, I've just got to tell you something!"

"Hold on, Jess," said the sleepy voice with a big yawn. "Don't you know it's only six o'clock on a Saturday morning? Have some pity."

"It's just the most unbelievable thing!"

"You sound like you've been to an all-night party," quipped Trish. Trish was really awake now. Her humor was returning.

"I'm at Nick's house," said Jessie.

"Oh?" said Trish in *that* tone of voice. Jessie could just imagine her raising those bushy black eyebrows of hers that she always said made her look like Groucho Marx. "I've seen you two together. I knew it was bound to get hot and heavy one of these days."

"No, no, no!" said Jessie, feeling a flush creep up her neck. So many astonishing things had been going on that she had forgotten. Nick had kissed her for the first time last night on the old pier. And she had liked it. But she didn't have time to think about that now.

"It's not Nick. It's that girl I saw on the beach yesterday. She's here at Nick's house right now," Jessie said.

There was a long pause on the other end of the phone. In the background Jessie could hear Dot's excited voice, "What's going on, Trish? Is anything wrong?"

"All right, Jess. I'm not laughing. It's not a very good joke," Trish finally said.

"I'm serious," Jessie said. "Nick's parents brought her home from their cruise. Their ship fished her out of the sea or something."

"Sure, sure, and I found a million dollars on the beach yesterday. Let me talk to Nick," came that self-confident, disbelieving voice that was Trish. She sounded cynical.

Jessie's stomach clenched. "Ah . . . you can't right now. He's downstairs, you know, with his parents and Marina. I'm using the phone upstairs in Nick's room."

"Is that her name — Marina? Or did you just make it up?" said Trish. "Now, come on! You're pulling my leg. If you don't let me talk to Nick and quit spoofing me I'm going to hang up."

"Trish, you wouldn't believe what's been going on here," Jessie said very low, running her hand through her hair. "I'm worried about Nick."

She turned and looked out the window at the sea crashing against the beach in the bright sunshine. None of this was real. None of it was happening to her. She took a deep breath to calm herself and told herself everything would be all right the minute she saw Trish.

From the moment Marina had entered the house, everyone began to act weird. Mrs. Stieveson had pretended it was the most natural thing in the world for Jessie to be sleeping on the sofa in their living room. She hadn't yelled at Nick or even raised her voice. Instead of calling Jessie's parents to tell them to come and get their daughter, she called Mrs. Rogers first thing and smoothed matters over. Mrs. Stieveson even explained that Jessie was something of a heroine. The girl that she had tried to fish out of the sea had survived largely due to Jessie's efforts. Jessie had kept her afloat long enough to give her air until the ship passed by in the storm and found her.

Such news had not elated Jessie as much as she thought it would. Nick's mother bustled about the house opening drapes and window shades at an alarming pace. She pulled out her best crystal and china before six in the morning and opened up cans of caviar and pots of cheese dips. She even broke out a bottle of champagne.

Dr. Stieveson, who was usually quite a talker, acted just the opposite. He collapsed into a rocking chair and barely moved. He let his eyes follow his wife around the kitchen and living room as she gave directions to her daughters, who moved at a sleepwalker's pace. Nick's father, the doctor, appeared haggard and drawn with a deathly white face and tired eyes with dark bags under them. He looked as if he had been through an ordeal that he didn't want to talk about.

Marina watched silently and smiled.

And Nick . . . Nick was the worst of all. As soon as he laid eyes on Marina, he backed away and would have nothing to do with her.

His mother chided him, "Nick, I hope I taught you better manners than that!" when he refused to be introduced or shake Marina's hand.

For a minute Jessie had feared he was going to run out of the house, get into his Saab, and zoom away. Jessie even saw him reach for his car keys. It was only when he caught the look of alarm on her face that he stuffed them back into his pocket and moved to her side. He wouldn't listen to any of his mother's directions to fetch a dessert plate out of the china cabinet or to pull up a chair for "poor Marina," who must be very tired and weak after her "horrifying ordeal." Nick merely stood in the corner — close to Jessie — with his hands jammed in his jeans pockets. He acted as if he didn't belong there anymore.

Marina followed everyone about the room with her eyes. She calmly took everything in — not just the people but the objects. She made her way about the living room, picking up all sorts of gadgets and studying them as if she had never seen them before. They all seemed to delight her — the television's remote control, a digital clock, a cigarette lighter, and the stereo system with the big speakers. But as soon as she started turning knobs on the stereo, Nick stepped in front of it, pushing her hands aside. Her blue eyes met his and held. Nick turned away first and went back to his corner.

Jessie had felt so confused and out of place that she had excused herself, pretending to go to the bathroom. Then she'd snuck upstairs to Nick's room — he had a separate phone line — and called Trish. Trish's humor always calmed her, and only Trish would know what to do.

"Jess, it'll be all right," said Trish after listening to her story. "I'll tell you what. Let's meet in the park right away."

"Yes, yes," said Jessie, feeling a great weight being lifted off her shoulders, "the park." She even felt the beginning of a smile.

"Just give me a chance to shower, dress, and grab a quick . . ."

Jessie was no longer listening. A white hand with slender fingers and long, pale fingernails had closed over Jessie's own hand, the one that was holding the telephone. Jessie spun around.

"I really wanted to thank you for helping me. You saved my life." Marina smiled at her. Her voice sounded as clear as crystal and just as smooth, just like the voice Jessie had heard yesterday. But Jessie was not aware of the voice as much, at least not after she met Marina's eyes. They were the same limpid blue, like the ocean. At times they sparkled like sunlight scintillating off the surface of the sea. Always they were deep — and Jessie could not look away. Never had she seen eyes like that before.

The voice on the phone was getting farther and farther away. "I'll even make a picnic lunch. That'll cheer you up, Jess," said Trish. "Dot'll make her ham salad. Jess, are you there? Do you hear me? I swear, if this is all one big joke, I'll — "

The phone clicked back down into its cradle before Jessie was aware of what she had done.

"You're welcome," Jessie said to Marina. "But I didn't do anything special — only what anybody else would have done."

"Very few people would be so courageous," Marina said. "Why, you nearly died for me."

A few hours later Jessie could not understand why she'd panicked. It seemed silly and childish to run upstairs to call Trish for help when no help was needed. Nick might be in a "mood" and his father might act as if he had indigestion, but that was not going to spoil her day. She was actually beginning to enjoy herself.

After Jessie got over what she chalked up to shyness and nervousness over the unusual circumstances, she found herself as fascinated with Marina Jacobsen as she had been with the girl on the surfboard. Marina was a talkative girl and just as likeable as she was pretty. The two girls spent the morning on the beach in front of Nick's house, coming in for lunch when Mrs. Stieveson called them. It seemed that they had everything — and anything — to talk about.

Marina had many questions to ask. That was only natural because she remembered nothing about her past. Jessie couldn't believe that a girl who had nearly drowned and couldn't even remember her name, let alone where she was from or who her parents were, could be so cheerful. Perhaps she really had hit her head on the board harder than Jessie imagined! If it hadn't been for the bracelet with her name engraved on the inside that Dr. Stieveson had found, no one would know her name was Marina Jacobsen.

Marina wanted to know everything about everything — where she was, who Jessie and the Stievesons were, and all there was to know about Virginia Beach. Marina was particularly interested to learn about Jessie's love of swimming. The one fact about her past that Marina could remember was being a swimmer. She made Jessie repeat again and again how she had seen her surfing to shore yesterday. It didn't seem to bother her that she'd been surfing right before she almost drowned.

"Yes, I think I can remember. I think I can see myself," she said excitedly. Those blue eyes shone.

Jessie felt needed. Marina clearly wanted her as a friend. Jessie was ashamed she had run away at first. She didn't know what had come over her. All she knew was that now in Marina's presence everything seemed right.

"You can take me to school with you on Monday." Marina cocked her head and gazed at Jessie with her turquoise-blue eyes. "Then you can show me your pool in the gym." When Jessie looked surprised, Marina said, "Oh, I forgot to tell you! Mrs. Stieveson has been so kind. She's invited me to stay with her until my parents are found." She flashed one of her most winning smiles at Nick's mother as one of his sisters brought her a drink of water.

Mrs. Stieveson seemed to dimple all over as she smiled back. "I guess I'll just be one of the gang," Marina shrugged.

"Sounds great," Jessie said. She ignored Nick's frown. He stood in the driveway washing his Saab while he kept his eye on her. When he thought Marina wasn't looking, he signaled Jessie to excuse herself and come over so he could talk to her. Well, Jessie wasn't about to talk to him! He could stew, for all she cared. She didn't like the way he was treating her new friend. She even agreed with Nick's mother. He was just being rude.

For a moment she actually wondered why he was being so obnoxious. It wasn't like him. He was usually the most polite of boys, and not like some of the other jerks at the high school who were always goofing off. When he started to come toward her, signaling even harder, he had such a look of pain on his face that she almost went to him.

"Jessie, is something wrong?" Marina asked.

"Oh, nothing! Nothing at all." She turned away from Nick. When she was around Marina, it was hard to pay attention to anyone else.

Trish and Dot showed up on the Stievesons'

doorstep in record time. Dot looked ashen pale. She was even biting her fingernails as she glanced first at Dr. Stieveson, then at Mrs. Stieveson, and lastly at Nick. When Mrs. Stieveson gushed over her and asked her if she wanted a Popsicle or an ice cream bar, she looked as if she was going to faint. Dot could barely be heard as she shook her head and mumbled, "No thanks."

Jessie introduced everybody. Trish took one look at Marina and said, "Jess, don't you think I ought to take you home now? Your mom's going to be worried." She stuck out her lip in grim determination. Her face was drained of all emotion. She was concentrating so hard she'd even remembered to put on two matching shoes this morning.

"That's what I've been trying to tell her all morning." Nick's red head suddenly popped up from nowhere. He had been working on his car and was now wiping his greasy hands on a wet cloth. Trish and Nick exchanged glances while Dot stared straight at Jessie and Marina in horror. A glimmer of understanding seemed to pass between Trish and Nick.

Jessie could feel herself go hot with resentment. Nick must have been talking to Dot and Trish in the driveway, and they had decided to gang up on her. Jessie couldn't even imagine what Nick must have said about Marina to make Dot look at the girl as if her eyes were going to pop out. And Jessie thought they were her friends!

Marina at least had better manners. She smiled, turned away, and began examining Mrs. Stieveson's tape deck.

"I've got a better idea," Jessie snapped. "Since everyone is intent on not getting along, why don't you three go off somewhere and leave us alone? Everyone will probably be happier that way."

Nick, Trish, and Dot stared at Jessie for a moment as if they didn't know her. Dot mumbled some excuse, and she and Trish disappeared. Nick lingered a moment longer before he went back to fixing his car.

Finally Jessie's mother called back. Jessie had to go home. Even Mrs. Stieveson couldn't put it off any longer. Trish and Dot were long gone. Jessie didn't have much choice but to look angry when Nick's red head popped up again and he motioned her over to his waiting Saab. The engine was already running. He obviously didn't want to waste a moment.

Nick pulled Jessie into the front seat beside

him. He was so excited he was breathing hard. At the touch of his hand she wanted to draw back. His hand was cold, ice cold. "Jess, we've got to go somewhere and talk. Maybe we could just drive around. I've been talking to my father and — "

"Jessie! Excuse me, but I've just remembered something." Marina hurried up to the car. Her legs were the longest Jessie had ever seen on a girl. She resembled a woman athlete with such a stride. She looked just like one of the gold medalists in the Olympics Jessie had seen in *Sports Today,* the ones Jessie most admired. Everything about Marina was totally fascinating.

Marina put her hand on the car door latch. "The day of the accident — was I wearing a necklace?"

"Yes!" Jessie turned around in her seat, remembering. "I have it in my bedroom. A diver found it and gave it to me. The crystal with the turquoise center looked so valuable I kept it and — "

Marina got into the backseat. "Good. I'll ride over to your house and get it. Nick can bring me back. That is, if he doesn't mind."

"Nick?" Jessie said aghast. He was gripping the steering wheel so tightly with both hands that his knuckles were turning white. He was clenching his teeth and grinding them together. Not liking Marina was one thing, being rude was another.

"Nick, can you hear me?" Jessie grasped his arm and shook it.

"I'm afraid you'll have to find another driver, Jess." He turned off the ignition, unbuckled his shoulder harness, and started to get out of the car. "I don't want any part of this."

Jessie was about to spit out, "Thank you, but I'll call a cab," when she caught sight of Marina sitting in the backseat with her hands folded on her lap, looking very unhappy. The poor girl had been through enough. She needed a break. Jessie had to do this for Marina's sake.

She grabbed Nick by the hand. "Please, Nick," she said, "please do it just for me."

Nick glowered at her. "All right, Jess, have it your way." Nick slammed the door shut and started the motor again.

Jessie was soon sorry she'd asked him. Nick was usually a cautious driver. He had made the best grade in the class when he took driver's education. Now he acted as if he were somebody else.

He pushed the gas pedal to the floor and

threw Jessie back against her seat as they zoomed down Atlantic Avenue. There weren't as many cars on the road on a Saturday in May — before the tourist season started — and he wove in and out of traffic, passing everyone in sight whether on the right or the left. He ignored the stop signs altogether. When he bothered to stop for a red light, he came to a screeching halt that threw her forward toward the dashboard. No sooner did he stop than he would start up again, making Jessie feel as if she were on an amusement park ride that never ended.

"Nick, what do you think you're doing!" Jessie screamed. "Do you want to get us all killed?" She bit her lip at the mention of the word "killed." Jessie looked back over her shoulder, but Marina was gazing out the window at the trucks and cars on the road. She didn't seem concerned in the least. Again Jessie assumed she was being polite.

But Nick didn't answer. He whipped down Pacific Avenue, nearly sideswiping a pickup truck loaded with watermelons. The driver pulled over to the side of the road, leaped out of the truck, and started shaking his fist and yelling at Nick.

Out of the corner of her eye, coming toward

them in the other lane, Jessie thought she recognized her father wearing his gray Virginia
Beach High sweatshirt with red letters. Yes,
it was him! He was riding in a van with the
high school sports coaches, coming back from
an end-of-the-school-year meeting at a local
country club.

Mr. Rogers picked her out in the front seat
at once. Her normally stern father looked even
more shocked when he spotted the driver. He
frowned at Jessie before Nick zipped past him,
and Jessie knew she would have hell to pay
for today. Nick was giving her a ride she was
going to regret to her dying day — if she lived
that long.

Jessie was clutching her seat and bracing
herself when they lurched up to the front of
the house and screeched to another halt, making black skid marks on the road. "All right,"
said Nick. "Here you are."

Jessie wondered if she should ask Marina
to come inside. She doubted whether she
should leave the girl in the car with Nick. He
had taken such a violent dislike to her, she
didn't know what he might do. She stood there
beside the car undecided, feeling nervous,
when Marina said, "You go get the necklace,

Jessie. I'll wait here. Then we won't delay Nick anymore." Marina smiled, and her blue eyes sparkled.

"All right. I'll be back in just a minute," Jessie promised. Marina's look calmed her. "I know just where I left it." As she ran into the house she barely noticed that the sky had a greenish, cloudy cast to it. The sunshine was gone. It looked odd somehow — different in a way that Jessie had never seen before. There was no wind. It was perfectly still.

Jessie quietly sneaked into the house. Her mother had been at home all day grading papers. She tiptoed past the living room where her mother was sitting on the sofa with her feet up on the coffee table and piles of history term papers surrounding her on every side. They were stacked so high they looked like the walls of a fort. Mrs. Rogers could barely see over the top. Jessie held her breath. If her mother saw her, she couldn't get the necklace for Marina.

"Jes-sie!" Her mother stood up, peering at her over her glasses.

Jessie froze in the hallway with her sneaker on the first stair. All was lost.

"Just what did you think you were doing

sneaking out of here last night after *I* was in bed? Especially after your behavior yesterday, I'm shocked at you."

"But, Mom, I'm just — "

"And what's this drivel about you saving a girl's life yesterday on the beach? You had no business on the beach and you know it. I'll not have you going around spreading tales of heroism."

"I didn't. That was Mrs. Stieveson's — "

"Upstairs to your room."

Mrs. Rogers started up the stairs after her.

"OK," Jessie said. Her mother was being stern even for her mother, and Jessie just didn't understand it. "But first I have to give something to Marina, something that belongs to her. You can even give it to her if you want. Just so long as she gets it."

"Maybe later. Right now you're going to your room." Her mother was not impressed. She herded Jessie upstairs.

"She's out in the car with Nick."

"This Nick of yours, I'm very disappointed in him. Your father just called me on his car phone. He said he saw you and Nick speeding down Pacific Avenue. He thinks Nick's parents ought to take away his car keys, just as we've taken away yours. For once I agree with him."

They had reached her room. Her mother was waving her inside.

"No, no, just wait a minute. I — "

"I don't want you to see Nick anymore."

The words, "I don't want you to see Nick anymore" reverberated through her mind like a pulsating throb of pain. Nick . . . She remembered what she had been blocking out of her mind all day, how he had held her in his arms last night and comforted her when she needed it.

He was sitting in the car in his strange mood, hurting inside. She had left him all alone. She was suddenly afraid for him. With a virtual certainty she knew something was wrong. She had to get to him, had to help. In one dizzying moment she forgot all about Marina.

"Mom, I've got to go. I'm sorry, but I've just got to!" Jessie shoved past her startled mother.

Years later Jessie could barely sort out the sequence of events that happened next.

At that moment there was a loud shattering of glass behind her as her bedroom window fell to pieces. The lights went out. Earlier in the day it had been sunny, but now it was as dark as night. A tremendous wind whipped through her bedroom, scattering her homework papers on her desk and knocking over a vase on her dresser that smashed on the floor. Outside she heard a loud cracking sound followed by a crash.

"Mom, Mom, where are you?" she called out as her heart thudded giddily against her chest. Her mother seemed to have disappeared. All the while she thought of Nick. He was outside in this storm.

She felt strangely disoriented in her own bedroom. She did not know where anything was as peal after peal of thunder boomed across the sky and shook the ground, rattling the very foundations of the house. Jessie groped for something familiar to guide her. Finally she found a wall and inched her way along to her dresser. It was impossible for it to be this dark in the afternoon in May. It was almost pitch black outside.

Jessie's hand landed on her jewelry box. It was turned over on its side with its contents spilled out. There was her brush, though her comb was gone. A bottle of perfume had shattered on the dresser top. She cut her finger on a shard of glass.

Her bed and the nightstand could not be far away now. She remembered exactly where they were located. She found her bed with the sheets half torn off, and then at last she bumped into her night table. There was the clock radio that had given her so much trouble the other night, but the necklace of shells with the crystal pendant had vanished. Marina would be devastated.

She wanted to search around on the floor for the pendant, but some inner certainty told her it would be a waste of time. It was gone. She would never find it.

And Nick . . . Jessie put her hand over her heart to still its beating. She had to get to Nick. She couldn't delay another second. If only the darkness and the wind would go away. Her knees felt like jelly, and she could barely walk.

It seemed to take an eternity for her to grope her way out of the bedroom and into what she recognized as the hallway. She nearly tripped over several paintings that had fallen to the floor.

Now think, Jess, she told herself. *Be careful or you'll never get to Nick.* She sat down and inched her way along the carpet. It was impossible to tell where the stairs began.

She found herself going down step by step. Gradually the darkness brightened, and she could begin to see again. Sirens wailed past on the streets outside. Other houses must have been hit by lightning very close by.

Finally at the bottom of the steps she could stand on her feet again. Her mother was trying to get through to the power company on the kitchen phone, but apparently even the phone lines were dead. Nothing stopped Mrs. Rogers. She tried again and again. Jessie was just relieved she was all right.

Jessie threw open the front door. At first she didn't take in what she was seeing. A crowd was gathered around the spot where Nick's Saab used to be. An old oak tree in the front yard had toppled over in the short, violent storm. Jessie was drawn to the sight step by step, but with each step it got harder to breathe.

The neighbors were all whispering, "It was a tornado. Did you see it? We get violent storms, but I've never seen a twister around here."

"It touched down at the end of the street, and it came so close to the Rogerses' house."

Jessie saw that whatever it was had run an eccentric path down the street, zigzagging back and forth across the road and knocking down trees all over the place. But her eyes were riveted to that place on the curb where Nick's Saab had been parked.

"An ambulance! Someone call an ambulance," screamed her next-door neighbor running back toward her house. The look on her face was one of sheer terror.

That terror showed on the faces of the neighbors gathered in the street. "There's someone in that car," came the whisper echoed up and down the lines of people.

"How is it possible?" wailed another lady, wringing her hands as everyone else backed away from the car, horrified. "How could anybody survive in that — that squashed tin can?"

"Let me through!" said Jessie. She would not admit that Nick was dead. He just couldn't be. It was too cruel. She couldn't live with it. Not after she'd been so nasty to him today. Not after last night when he had kissed her for the first time.

There were so many things she intended to say to him after she got done being angry. And he had wanted to tell her something his father had said. Now it was hard to remember what she had been so irritated about. There was only the next day together, the next talk, the next drive that would not happen now. She would never see that red head with freckles and those green eyes smiling at her again. He would never again be waiting to drive her home from school — or anywhere.

"Look, it's Jessie." The neighbors moved away to make room, shaking their heads in pity. "Wasn't he her boyfriend?"

"Are you all right, honey?" said another, no doubt because she was so pale. Jessie gaped at the smashed-in black car with the tree lying on top of it. She knew she had to look in there.

As soon as she reached for the door latch she heard it. "Jessie!" came her mother's voice from the doorway. Mrs. Rogers's voice was filled with dread and warning. She shook her head. "Don't go over there." Her mother had never looked more terrified. She put her hand to her throat.

"I've got to." Jessie swallowed hard. "There isn't much time," she blurted out. She was prompted by some instinct she didn't understand.

Jessie opened the door and looked inside the crushed black box that used to be a Saab. She was tensed and poised, ready for something even worse to happen. Her heartbeat kept time with her urgency. It grew faster and faster. She groped in the dark until she felt a human body on the floor in what used to be the front seat. There was only one body. Marina was gone. Jessie checked the backseat just to be sure.

Jessie tugged at Nick with all her strength. Something exploded first in her mind before it exploded inside the car engine. With superhuman effort, Jessie yanked Nick from the wreckage and back into her yard. The car burst into flames with an explosion that could be heard blocks away.

Chapter 6

Nick could remember little about the accident when he woke up in Norfolk Memorial Hospital on the Chesapeake Bay side of Virginia Beach. He knew only that every bone in his body felt broken. He hurt everywhere. The doctors said he had been lucky. He had escaped without serious injury. A few of his ribs were cracked. He had a broken left arm, but he was right-handed so it didn't even interfere with writing. Other than that, he had suffered only a mild concussion that he recovered from rapidly.

He was eager to leave the hospital. He could see more of Jessie that way. At Norfolk Memorial Hospital she could visit only during hours that weren't reserved for family and only when Dr. and Mrs. Rogers would let her come. After they had found out Nick was going to live, they tried to keep Jessie away. She sneaked in at odd times — after work at the pool, after school, and right before she went home for dinner. But Marina had been keeping her away more and more often. Nick knew it.

Nick had time on his hands. He remembered again and again the events that terrible Saturday afternoon. . . .

Marina had been sitting so silently in the backseat of his Saab that Nick had been unable to bear it. He had not intended to say anything until Jessie came back with the necklace, but he couldn't help himself. He felt that somehow Marina was deliberately provoking him.

"You think you're very clever, don't you?" Nick gripped the steering wheel. "Well, you don't fool me. You don't fool my father, either, though he's too upset to say so to your face. He said I wouldn't believe everything he knew about you. He's wrong. *I would.*"

Tensely Nick waited for Marina to answer. But she did not even open her mouth. He knew she was there. He could feel her evil presence like a kind of heat glowing there behind him, scorching him. She was loathsome, just like a slug he had once picked off the underside of a rock.

"I know what you are thinking." Nick would not be intimidated. "You plan to turn Jessie against me. I don't know why, but I'll find out. I swear to you, if you hurt her it will be the last thing you do."

Again the girl said nothing. Nick heard no sound but his own breathing, and that was ragged enough. "You can't turn Jessie against me, you know. We've known each other forever. We grew up together. She likes me — almost as much as I like her."

Marina remained mum.

This was the last straw. The creature was no doubt up to some trick. Nick spun around to confront her. She was ready and waiting for him — with a smile. The smile appeared unearthly in its brilliance. When she stared directly into his eyes with her own very blue ones, he felt himself losing sense of time and place. He began to forget who he was and even worse to forget his anger at her, thinking she wasn't so bad after all and perhaps he was mistaken about her.

Nick felt to his very core that this was how she took advantage of others and fooled them. But he was a Stieveson. He was different. He knew better. Nick resisted her power, put the brakes on, in a sense, and came to another skidding halt. For a blinding moment, he forced himself to close his eyes and shut her out.

A German shepherd was on his way down the sidewalk when the dog caught sight of Nick's car with the windows rolled down. He stopped and sniffed. The dog bared his teeth and put back his ears. He growled and barked viciously.

It was then that Nick's eyes popped open. He took in Marina's smile and gaze again. This time he saw more clearly. Behind the smile was a smirk. Those clear blue eyes were laughing at him — mocking him.

"All right, you monster, out of my car!" Nick hollered. "Get away from me and get away from Jessie." He reached back to grab her shoulder and shake her.

At that moment the odd-colored, green-tinted sky overhead seemed to explode. A violent wind whipped past the car. The oak tree overhead came crashing down. Nick ducked. After that he remembered nothing at all until he woke up in the hospital — except Marina's last malevolent look.

Nick had to get well. He had to get back to school. Marina was in school all day with Jessie while he was lying flat on his back in bed.

Nothing was worse than his dread of Marina. He didn't trust her, not for a minute. He had no doubt she had tried to kill him in the storm, but not as an end in itself. Marina wanted him out of the way to get to Jessie. But *why, why, why?* If Marina wanted to kill Jessie, it would be easy. She obviously wanted something else. But what? He had to find out before Jessie discovered for herself that some things could be worse than death.

Dot and Trish came to visit him, too. They gave him valuable information. They seemed to be the only other ones in school or in Virginia Beach, for that matter, who weren't overly impressed with Marina Jacobsen.

Trish told him that Marina had returned to the Stievesons' house alone, on foot, and in tears that Saturday while everyone was in a pandemonium about Nick. She claimed to have been hit on the head in the storm. She did not remember anything about how she got out of the car before the tree collapsed.

Nor did she have an explanation why she acted unconcerned about the necklace that had been lost in the storm. Marina didn't put an ad in the papers. She didn't call the police. She seemed to forget all about the shell necklace with the crystal with the turquoise center. But her right eye glowed all the brighter when anyone asked about it.

Mrs. Stieveson welcomed Marina and called her "daughter" while she was going to the hospital every day to be with Nick. Of course Marina didn't visit him. She stayed home, did dishes, and helped with chores. Everyone thought Marina was such a good girl. Nick knew better. He knew she hadn't lost any sleep over him. She was just lying low and plotting how to kill him off the next time.

Nick was overjoyed when the doctor X-rayed him for the last time and told him he could go home. "But you'll have to stay in the house for at least two weeks — just to see if complications develop. And when you go back to school — no swimming!"

Two weeks near the end of his senior year was an impossible amount of time to sacrifice. The big swim meet was in two weeks. Even he was almost ready to admit he couldn't swim with a broken arm — almost. He said "almost" because Marina had caused it, and he didn't want to give her any easy victories.

But Nick was smart. He agreed to everything just to get out of the hospital.

"We hope your father's feeling better. We even hope to see Dr. Stieveson back to work soon." Nick's doctor turned at the door.

"He will be," said Nick, sticking up his chin. No one was going to keep a Stieveson down forever, especially not Marina. Whatever she was.

Yet Nick was soon to discover just how badly off his father really was. He shared the house with him during the day in a kind of mutual convalescence. Nick tried to find out exactly what his father knew about Marina. Yet every time he asked him, his dad merely opened up another can of beer and guzzled it down. His father had hardly touched the stuff before except for a can during baseball and football games. Now he was developing a regular beer belly.

"Dad, if you don't tell me what you know, we can't do anything about Marina," Nick pleaded, while his father sat in his rocking chair in the living room and stared off into space. It was painful to see him like this. This brilliant doctor who was nationally renowned didn't even bother to shave in the morning. When the phone rang with a call from a concerned colleague, Dr. Stieveson wouldn't even bother to answer it. He rarely even dressed except to put on old jeans and a work shirt.

"We can't do anything about her, anyway." His father's lips met in a grim line. He raised a can of beer and took a deep swallow.

"But why?"

His father shook his head.

Even worse, his mother seemed totally oblivious to the situation, as did his sisters. They bustled about the house telephoning friends, holding parties, and above all entertaining Marina. Marina held them under a spell. His mother called his father's condition "a little cold" and could not see disaster hanging over them. Nick would not get his family back until he got rid of Marina.

When Nick wasn't catching up on his homework, he searched Marina's room. There was precious little else to do besides watch baseball games with his dad. But she had left depressingly few clues.

Nick was getting so impatient and bored that he went searching for a pack of cards to play solitaire. He thought it might calm him down and help him think more clearly. He opened the old rolltop desk in the living room, the one his father had used to pay bills. Out fell a leather briefcase.

For a moment Nick didn't recognize it. His father used to have so many briefcases for different occasions. Then he remembered it was the one his father had taken to the surgeons' convention in Bermuda. Judging from the way it was bulging, it had never been unpacked. It was still stuffed with papers. Nick supposed that in his father's present mood he had just thrown it aside when he came through the front door and had never looked at it again.

Nick sat down and unzipped it eagerly. Then he stopped, wondering if this was the right thing to do. But when he glanced over at his father drinking beer in front of the television set he knew anything was better than what he saw. Desperate measures were required. Anything that would help his family get back together was right. And he was certainly the only one to do it. No one else could even see what was happening.

There were sheaves of papers here all right. Most of them were printed handouts from the convention itself with lists of doctors and addresses of their practices. Other sheets concerned schedules for seminars and lists of parties and get-togethers on the ship during the Bermuda cruise. Still other packets of information advertised Bermuda itself — sight-seeing, shopping, restaurants, and beaches. Nick found undeveloped rolls of film and snapshots of his father, mother, and sisters together in the pool. Nothing here that one wouldn't expect to find in the briefcase of any conference participant.

Nick was almost sorry he had looked when at the very bottom of the pile he found a file of quite a different nature. He wouldn't have noticed it if it hadn't slipped out and fallen on the floor. It wasn't even labeled, but when the papers scattered he could see charts, graphs, and medical test results — all about Marina.

There was a virtual gold mine here — the mother lode. Much of the evidence he needed seemed to be compiled here in front of him. Of course Nick was no doctor, and most of the numbers meant nothing to him. He went for the notebook. Maybe the written record would explain everything else.

Much of it was in the form of a doctor's day-by-day journal. Up until the last day the events recorded were just regular conference seminars and notes. Nick was beginning to think all he would have to go by were the indecipherable medical reports that he would have to take to another physician to interpret. But then in the entry for the last day of the con-

ference he found what he was looking for —
and more than he was bargaining for as well.

Friday 4:30 P.M.

*Girl about age 17 was fished out of water with
nets after two passengers sighted her overboard
and screamed for help. 5 feet 11 inches in height,
about 140 pounds in weight. Blond hair, blue
eyes. Bracelet tag said her name was Marina
Jacobsen. Wearing swimsuit. No other identi-
fication.*

*Cardiopulmonary resuscitation and mouth-
to-mouth were performed on deck with no result.
Rushed to operating room aboard the ship and
doctors from all specialties called in. We have
a ship full of them! I was put in charge of the
team because of my experience in the emergency
trauma unit at Norfolk Memorial.*

*We worked on the girl for four hours straight
right through the late afternoon and early evening. It was the oddest case. Drowning victims
are usually blue in color, but she was only very
pale. Nor were her lungs filled with water. When
we pumped, nothing came out. We could find
no reason why she shouldn't be breathing, but
she wasn't.*

*There was no heartbeat nor any sign of one.
Her pulse could not be taken. Blood pressure*

was totally absent. At first we thought our equipment was malfunctioning. It would register nothing. Absolute zero. It was as if we were working on a wooden dummy instead of a human being. It reminded me of those old days in first-year medical school when we practiced on the cadavers, the ones that were cold and long dead.

The other physicians in attendance thought we should pack her up in ice and send her to the deep freeze. It was a peculiar case, one for the medical journals, but she was obviously dead. There must be no sign of decay because either she had just died or the cold seawater in the Atlantic had preserved her body.

We all consulted with each other, and everyone but me decided to give up the case. They were eager to attend the captain's ball that evening. They had already missed an afternoon's worth of conference events and wanted to get their money's worth before we docked in Norfolk again.

"Fly her to Norfolk Memorial and do an autopsy if you're curious!" one friend told me, clapping me on the back. "Don't waste your time tonight."

I wish I had followed his advice. Or better yet I wish I had forgotten about the case altogether, just like any other sane doctor. Then I would be ignorant of what I know now. I wouldn't possess this horrible knowledge that I've got to live with every day and then carry to the grave with me.

I decided to try one more test. You could call it the ultimate test to see if someone is truly dead or alive. I've known cases where blood pressure wouldn't register on clearly living, healthy persons. My patients and I have laughed about it. Ditto with the pulse. And people who haven't been breathing for a long time have been brought back to life, particularly if their bodies have been kept cold in the meantime. But I've never known a case where brain waves were absent and the person was alive.

I hooked her up to an electroencephalogram machine, of course expecting to find nothing so that my mind, too, could be at rest and I could join my wife and daughters for dinner and dancing. Much to my surprise, brain waves were present. Nor were they the brain waves of one dying on the operating table or even the brain waves of one asleep. They were the normal brain waves of a conscious, breathing person who was fully awake.

I was very tired from working six hours straight on this case, and my nerves were frayed.

I confess I gave way at that moment to un-professional behavior. I backed away from the operating table in horror, staring at her body for many moments before I could approach her again. My imagination was running away from me, and I thought I was sharing the room with some strange sort of unexplained creature who was taking in everything that I did. Did she hear my sharp intake of breath? I feared she saw me through those wide open, gaping eyes that stared at the ceiling. They seemed so intensely blue.

Then I shook myself. I must be very tired, more tired than I knew. The only explanation was that I had used the machine wrong or it was malfunctioning. Anything else my mind couldn't accept.

I gave orders for her body to be sent to the deep freeze to keep the corpse under refrigeration until we reached shore. I hoped I was done with the wretched case and it would bother me no more.

I had quite a bit to drink that night. I had an inkling I hadn't seen my last of her.

Friday — late — about midnight:
We'd all been dancing for hours. Nobody

wanted to go back to their cabins. Can't blame them after what we've been through today.

How did I know it even then? A flustered waitress tapped me on the shoulder and said there was someone just outside the dining room who wished to speak to me. The woman looked very confused and upset, so I did not ask any more questions. I grabbed my wife's drink and downed it before I excused myself.

There the girl was, standing on her own two feet just as I knew she would be. She put her hand to her head and looked at me with those intense blue eyes that I could see even in the darkness. "Dr. Stieveson," she said in a voice so clear it sounded like a crystal bell, "could you tell me where I am?"

"Who do we have here? Oh, poor thing!" My wife had followed me outside and proceeded to gush over the girl. If she hadn't shown up, I don't know what I would have done. I couldn't speak. I was lost from that moment.

The creature even knew my name.

Chapter 7

At first Jessie thought it would be hard to concentrate on her schoolwork when she was so worried about Nick. But Marina came to class with her starting on Monday. With Marina around she found school much easier than she had expected.

"After all, Nick's going to live," Marina reassured her. "I can guarantee that."

"But — "

"You spend too much time worrying about him," her new friend said as they climbed out of Trish's car.

Trish had called the night before and asked if she could drive everyone to school that week, considering the accident and all. But Dot's eyes kept shifting from Marina to Jessie and back again as if she were afraid to say anything. Trish kept silent the whole way to school — not one joke. That made Jessie wonder fleetingly what the sisters were up to. Jessie got the distinct impression that Dot was watching her in the backseat through her sun visor's mirror.

"See you later," Trish said pointedly to Jessie.

After the first morning back at school, Jessie was proud as well as happy to be Marina's friend. It was hard to imagine what was wrong with Trish and Dot. Everyone else liked the new girl. Were Trish and Dot jealous? Perhaps it was a case of sour grapes? Well, they would get over it.

Marina charmed all the teachers. She was the best student in almost every class, particularly English and history as well as foreign languages. She didn't seem to know much about science or math, though she spent most of her time in the lab just examining objects curiously as if she'd never seen them before. Of course it must be the effect of her amnesia from the near-drowning. Jessie, as well as the other students, paid no attention to her fascination with electric lights, Bunsen burners, and test tubes.

Even if she didn't know the first thing about

balancing an equation in chemistry class, her smile was bright enough to win over Mr. Snodgrass, the chemistry teacher. That alone was quite a sensation. To everyone's knowledge, no one in the history of Virginia Beach High School had ever won a smile from Mr. Snodgrass, let alone an open invitation to call him any time she needed help. Usually he scowled at all the students and wrote big red "F's" at the top of every worksheet or quiz. But this Monday he spent the whole class period asking Marina what she thought of Virginia Beach and inviting her to be their guest as long as she stayed with them.

The boys didn't even need an introduction. They went wild. Her leggy good looks and perfect figure not only made the girls whisper in corners with envy but made the rudest boys open doors when they saw Marina coming. Before lunch she must have had five invitations to the senior dance, and before the final bell had rung on Monday she had gotten five more dates — that is, if she had wanted to accept them. She turned them all down with her gracious smile, saying she wouldn't be here long.

Jessie held her hand over her mouth so no one would see her smile. She bet Marina was only being polite. None of these gawky fellows in T-shirts and blue jeans could possibly interest a girl of Marina's talents and skills.

Even the local newspapers — the *Virginia Times, The Daily Progress, The Gazette,* and *Virginia Beach Today* — had gotten the tip. They were at the school with the morning buses to interview her. The high school campus was laid out with outside walkways between the buildings. Every time Marina would emerge from a door, they would surround her like bees buzzing with questions. Her story appealed to them. The headlines read, "Girl from Nowhere Fished Out of the Sea" or "A Real Life Mermaid Comes to Virginia Beach."

Of course Marina's accounts of the near-drowning meant that the police never brought any charges against Jessie.

"How does it feel not to remember who you are or where your parents are from?" The KRRX-TV reporter held a mike up to Marina when she was headed to Trish's car at the end of the day.

Marina shrugged with total lack of concern. "I don't mind. I have found a new friend who is like a sister to me. Everyone is so nice."

Jessie blushed because she knew Marina meant her. No one so important had ever befriended her before.

Soon the story was in all the papers up and down the East Coast. Marina's picture appeared everywhere. Why her parents didn't claim her no one could understand, least of all Jessie. She just knew she was thankful for every day Marina could stay with them.

Jessie had told everyone so much about Marina's surfing skills that no one was absent from swim practice that day except Nick. They gathered around the pool expectantly to watch. Anyone who could surf that well had to be able to swim.

Marina's first racing dive into the pool was as perfect as Jessie had always imagined it would be — and as effortless. Everything she did always seemed to be easy for her. No one had called out a stroke for her to do. But after a fast glide underwater that took her almost halfway across the pool, she surfaced doing the breaststroke.

Somehow Jessie had known that would be Marina's stroke. It made her think of Nick and how this girl outclassed even him. Until today

Nick was the best she had ever seen. He already hated Marina. This would make him hate her and resent her even more.

Jessie didn't know how Nick could blame Marina for the tornado. The poor girl had been a victim, too. It seemed an ugly side of Nick's nature that Jessie had never suspected before, although she liked him so much in every other respect it was hard to hold it against him. She could only hope that someday Nick and Marina would learn to get along.

The swim coach met Marina at the end of ten laps to shake her hand as she came out of the pool. "Nick Stieveson used to hold the team record for the two-hundred-yard breaststroke. Now you do, young lady. Congratulations. Perhaps you can take his place in the big meet. You can be the one-hundred-yard breaststroker in the four-hundred-yard medley relay."

"Thank you," said Marina, beaming at everyone who crowded around to clap her on the back and congratulate her. "But I have a better idea. Why not Jessie?"

Instantly there was silence. There was not a sound in the entire pool area except the splashing of the water against the sides of the pool in Marina's wake. That soon died down to nothing. All eyes that had been focused on Marina now turned to Jessie in amazement.

Jessie felt a deep red flush creeping up her neck and coloring her cheeks crimson. She was no better than an average breaststroker with an unspectacular time. No matter how much she practiced, Jessie supposed she was meant to stay that way. She was "good, old dependable Jess" that the coach would always stick on the end lane of the pool. He placed her in the center lane only when their team was already winning. She had gotten used to never seeing her name in the school paper the day after a meet when the reporters discussed winning times.

The coach was speechless for a moment. Then he said, "I'll be glad to put Jessie in the center lane when she swims as fast as you."

"But she will. By the Saturday of the meet she'll be every bit as good as I am," Marina said with that smile that no one could resist.

The coach was so taken aback that he could do nothing but nod woodenly. He opened his mouth to speak. Yet he seemed to forget what he was going to say when he met her eyes.

"Marina." Jessie caught her by the arm after they had changed in the locker room and left the gym. "Why did you do that for me?"

"You saved my life, didn't you?" Marina tossed her blond locks over her shoulders.

"Well yes, I suppose I helped, but — "

"That's worth something, isn't it?"

"If you put it that way. But you didn't have to — "

"I want to."

Starting the next day Marina played coach while Jessie took time off from her job at the pool to practice after school. "This is so silly," said Jessie as she got into the pool. "I'll never be able to swim like you."

But Marina would not take "no" for an answer. The girl's presence infused Jessie with a sense of self-confidence she'd never felt before. It surged through her veins, lifting her to heights she had never dreamed possible. Somehow she just could not let Marina down.

Her first time out she did not do as well as Marina, but she improved her time. She did better than she had ever done before. "Do you want me to be your coach now?" Marina leaned over Jessie in the pool. "I think you could make a real splash in swimming circles."

Jessie could not believe her luck in finding Marina. She nodded.

Jessie did not know how she had the nerve

to do it, but on Marina's advice she quit her job at the pool. When the last bell had rung, they hopped into Jessie's car (Marina had persuaded her to do without Trish's chauffeur services, since Jessie's parents didn't seem to mind if Marina drove) and headed for the high school pool. If it was full, they drove to the next school or even a public pool if nothing else could be found.

Jessie had never felt so flattered. Her time improved steadily as Marina worked for hours with her on refining her arm and leg action and then on synchronizing the whole stroke. Jessie began to think she must be imposing. "I won't bother you anymore after the meet," Jessie said. "I'll do well, but I won't win. Then things will go back to normal."

"You give up too easily," said Marina. "There are lots of summer competitions. And who knows? You could try for the Olympic team."

Jessie had always dreamed of being in the Olympics. This was like a dream come true. If she pinched herself she might wake up. After that Jessie devoted herself entirely to her swimming and did whatever Marina suggested.

No one seemed quite so special as her friend. Marina had made Jessie into a new person. Far from being tired from all the physical exertion, Jessie found Marina's directions seemed to expand her energy level and improve her endurance. Jessie even did better in class. Marina had made her feel as if she could do anything at all if she put her mind to it. The girl had awakened new powers Jessie never suspected she possessed. As an added bonus, at night Jessie now went to sleep without a second thought. No more did she feel a suffocating sensation as if a black weight were pressing in on her lungs. She was free.

"But, Marina," she said after one day's workout, "why don't you enter the Olympic competition?"

Marina said lightly, "We don't even know who I am for sure, remember? Shall the announcer say, 'The girl from nowhere in lane five'?"

Both girls laughed.

"Seriously," said Marina in that pearly voice of hers, "I'd rather be a coach. It suits me better to work behind the scenes." She looked at Jessie, and her eyes glinted blue.

Jessie tried to console her friend. So far the police could turn up nothing. No leads. No clues. But Marina had to belong somewhere. "They'll find your parents soon."

"The doctors say my amnesia could be permanent. Something to do with my brain cells." She smiled. Marina took everything in her stride. It seemed impossible for her to get upset.

Marina worked a kind of magic. The girl had only to command, and Jessie could do. Jessie never got away with saying she couldn't. When Marina was around, she always could.

"It's Nick." Her mother held the phone out to her when she came through the door after spending the afternoon with Marina at the pool. Her mother did not seem to like either Nick or Marina. She was scowling at Jessie worse than usual these days.

Jessie took the phone guiltily. She had not been calling Nick much recently. She had been far too busy to remember. But then that seemed strange — too busy to call Nick.

"Hello, Nick, how are you?" Jessie said.

"Let's get over the 'hello Nick' stuff, Jess. I've got far more important things to talk about. I don't like to mention them over the phone. Can you come over tomorrow after school?"

"Tomorrow after school? I can't. I've got swim practice with Marina." Jessie hadn't told Nick about her pact with Marina on purpose. Now her secret was out.

There was dead silence on Nick's end. "Don't you think you've spent too much time with her lately? She's not the best influence, you know."

"I don't know what you're talking about. Besides, it's none of your business what I do, Nick Stieveson."

He took a deep breath, "Look, Jess, I'm just thinking of you. Promise you won't see Marina again until you've talked to me first. She's dangerous. I know things about her that would make your skin crawl."

Jessie slammed the phone down and wouldn't answer when it immediately rang again. It didn't matter if it rang thirty-six times. She had to teach Nick a lesson. He couldn't talk like that about her best friend.

The next day Dot and Trish waved at her as they passed on the walkways at school changing classes. "Long time, no see," quipped Trish. "Thought you'd turned into a fish, you're in the water with Marina so much these days."

"Knock it off, Trish," Jessie said.

But when she thought of Nick, there was always a nagging doubt at the back of her mind that she couldn't define.

Marina seemed to read her mind one day. "I don't think you should see Nick so much."

"But why? We have our disagreements, but I guess I still like him."

"You're practicing so much you don't have time for him." The girl frowned. For the first time Jessie saw an ugly look cross Marina's unblemished, pale face. "He's no good for you."

"Oh?"

"He's jealous of your success. He doesn't want you to beat his time. He'll keep you back."

It was true that today she'd beaten Nick's record. She'd never thought about it quite like that before. Yet somehow it didn't seem right. That didn't sound like Nick. Lately her thoughts were confused, and she'd had trouble thinking straight. When she attempted to ponder what was going on, her head hurt. She gave up trying.

Whenever Nick called, Jessie told her mother to say she wasn't at home. It was just too painful to be with him anymore. He did nothing but argue with her. When Jessie was around Marina, she always felt good.

"Jessie, are you feeling all right lately?" her mother asked.

"Yes, yes, of course. I'm fine."

"You're not acting like yourself."

"I'm not my old self, Mom. I feel like somebody different."

"I suppose so." Mrs. Rogers looked up at her doubtfully from her stack of term papers.

It was Friday, the day before the big swim meet. No one would admit Nick back to school. His doctor said he was not to return until next week at the earliest. Mrs. Stieveson had made sure everyone understood — from the principal, to the school secretary, to the janitor. So when Nick "borrowed" his father's Cadillac while no one was looking and drove over to the high school after lunch, he couldn't even sneak back into class. His rib cage was all wrapped up in bandages, and he walked kind of stiffly with his arm in a sling. No one could miss him. He stood out like The Mummy.

Before Nick was dismissed again, he left a note on Jessie's locker. He knew there was scant chance she would answer it. She had managed to ignore him lately with the help of that creature who was always following her about like a guardian evil spirit.

"Poor Nick!" Marina seemed to appear out of nowhere. She managed to look self-possessed and cool even in one of his sisters' dresses. But then Marina seemed very good at stealing things that didn't belong to her, like clothing, houses, and lives.

Here was something new. It was hard for Nick to meet her gaze. Before it had been compelling, but now it was almost blinding. Nick put his hand up to shield his face. The light seemed to come from her right eye. The blue of her eye looked astonishingly like the turquoise jewel embedded in the center of the crystal, the one on the necklace lost in the storm.

Marina snatched the note from the locker before Nick, in his bandaged state, could stop her. "I'll deliver it for you," she hissed.

Nick knew just how likely it was that Jessie would ever see his note.

Nick was not a quitter. That's what had made him lead breaststroker on the swim team. As soon as school let out he intended to call Jessie's house.

While Nick was driving home through the Friday afternoon traffic he turned on his dad's CB radio to see what he could pick up. But instead of truck drivers, today it seemed to be two policemen.

"Find anything on that girl that nearly drowned at the beach?" one said.

Nick listened closely and turned up the volume.

"Naw, I've been looking all week. The darned Bureau of Vital Statistics doesn't have anything on her — no birth certificate, no nothing."

"We've been checking across the country for missing person reports. Nothing corresponds to her description."

"But she couldn't have just come from nowhere. I — "

Nick turned the radio off. Grimly he raced home and dialed Jessie's number again. Not that he thought she would talk to him, but this time he'd have to warn Mrs. Rogers about Marina. It wasn't likely she'd believe him, but Nick was desperate.

"Hello?" came the harsh, schoolmarm voice.

"Mrs. Rogers, it's Nick. You've got to talk to Jessie for me. She's in terrible danger . . ."

He started to pour out the whole convoluted mess he'd read in his father's conference papers. Nick never realized how crazy it sounded until he heard it aloud.

She interrupted him right away. "Teenagers these days! I think you've seen too many horror movies, young man. If I catch you coming near my daughter again, I'll call the police! I — " Then her voice cracked with what sounded like a sob as she hung up.

Nick had expected the anger but not the fear in her tone. Mrs. Rogers really sounded scared. She was a tough lady. Nothing frightened her, at least nothing before today.

But Nick would put up with any amount of abuse to reach Jessie. He tried calling once more to reason with Mrs. Rogers. This time he got the answering machine. He waited impatiently to leave a message, tapping his fingers on the kitchen table. "You have reached the Rogers residence," came Jessie's recorded voice. "No one can come to the phone right now. If you will leave your name, num — " Then her voice broke off.

The message stopped midsentence. Someone had picked up the phone. He could hear breathing.

"Jessie?" he said. "Jessie, is it you?"

She didn't answer. Again he heard only breathing.

"Who is it? What have you done with Jessie?" he insisted. He felt the presence of something evil.

Nick heard a "click." He was disconnected.

Chapter 8

As soon as he hung up, Nick dashed over to Jessie's house in his father's Cadillac. It was nearing rush hour. Nick drove as fast as the swelling traffic, his cracked ribs, and one hand on the steering wheel would allow. He was certain something terrible was about to happen. That presence on the phone . . . that feeling of evil . . .

He found a frosty Mrs. Rogers with her hair up in a bandanna and curlers doing housework.

"Is Jessie all right?" he asked.

"I thought I told you to leave my daughter alone. I — "

Nick pushed past her. He heard Jessie's voice.

Jessie and Marina sat in the living room working math problems. "Jessie, has anything happened?" Nick stopped in front of her.

"Nick, this really is the outside of too much!. I told you before you're not my keeper. You don't have to follow me around like this."

It was obvious that Jessie really did not want to talk to him. Marina gave him her most mysterious smile when the creature glanced up from her page of analytical geometry.

That witch was the one who'd picked up the phone. Nick knew it. Marina was boasting of her power over Jessie — but her power to do what?

"All right, Jess," he conceded, "but if you need me just call."

It was infuriating. There was obviously something going on that Nick didn't know about — and he was going to discover what it was if it killed him. He felt so down and gloomy that he drove his dad's car to the Lynnhaven Mall and just walked around. He rode up and down the escalators and got lost in the mobs of late afternoon shoppers. Somehow the crowds helped him think.

"Nick!" called a familiar voice. He scanned the crowd of shoppers coming toward him. A head of black, wavy curls bobbed above everyone's packages and backpacks. "You look like a train just ran you over and then came back and did it again," said Trish, popping out of the crowd with her sister Dot beside her.

Dot was carrying enough packages to hide all but her anxious voice and her ponytail bouncing behind her. "Is that Nick?"

"Wow!" Trish looked Nick over with concern. "Let's go to the Burger Palace where we can talk."

"It's Jessie," Nick sighed while Dot went to get a triple order of double cheeseburgers, large fries, and chocolate milk shakes. He told Trish everything. Days seemed to have turned into years. Trish did not interrupt him nor did her expression change as she listened. Nick was certain Jessie's friend would laugh at him when he told her what Marina was. If Trish made one joke he knew he would probably flip out.

But she didn't. When he finished there was silence. Trish stared into her cup and occasionally stirred her milk shake with her straw. "I believe it," Trish finally said, astounding Nick. "I knew there was something not quite right from the first time I saw her. When I brush against her in the halls, her skin always feels cold. If you look at her fingernails, there's no color underneath. She never blushes or tans. She's *always* chalk white."

"And she's always in the pool!" Dot leaned her head in toward Nick and Trish and whispered. "I saw her in the pool the other day during lunch when it was closed and the teachers weren't even there. How did she get in there? She can't seem to stay away."

"There's even something odd about her right eye lately." Trish screwed up her face and shook her head. "It seems to give off a weird light. When you look at it you have to turn away. It's just too bright."

"I think it's the crystal from the necklace that got lost in the storm," said Nick. "Marina's put it back where it belongs. Maybe it took her all these decades to find it after the shipwreck when she went down with Captain Olaf Stieveson. Of course, you know she's really Lady Ingrid?"

Trish swallowed hard, paling. She nodded. "I gathered that."

"Who knows? Maybe she spotted Jess first. Maybe she was just coming to shore when Jess spotted her that awful day." Nick shrugged. "But Marina risked losing the crystal again when she pretended to drown. She's so evil she just couldn't resist working her spell on Jess right away — whatever it is."

"Now that she's found the eye," shuddered Dot, "her terrible powers must be back to full strength."

"That's why I can't get near Jess," Nick said. "That witch is keeping me away."

"Oh, poor Jess!" Dot said, biting her nails. "Marina's probably with her now!"

Nick felt all the color drain from his face. But Dot was right. They had to do something. Right away.

The three of them agreed to split up that Friday evening. Trish and Dot took the Cadillac instead of Trish's car because it had a car phone. Nick was to ride home on the bus.

"Are you sure your dad won't mind?" said Dot.

"He's so far out of it he doesn't know anything," said Nick. "He'll never miss it. He never leaves the house. And Mom walks around in a fog."

"We'll give you half an hour to get home and then let you know where Jess is. If she leaves her house, we'll try to keep a safe distance." Trish took the car keys.

"Good. Marina's bound to be less suspicious of you than me," Nick said. "Thanks."

At first everything went according to plan. The phone was ringing when Nick entered the kitchen.

"It's slow going," said Trish. "No one's left her house since we got here. We're parked at the end of the block."

Dot grabbed the phone from her sister. "We called our mom and told her we were spending the night at a friend's house. That way we can call out for pizza and camp out here all night if we have to."

"Keep up the good work," said Nick. "I'm going to talk to my father — now."

Nick watched his father sitting in front of the television in his old work clothes holding a can of beer. His eyes seemed glazed over and tired; his mind was far away. He didn't even notice when Nick flicked off the television.

"Dad." He pulled up a stool. "We've got to talk." Nick was certain his father still knew something the rest of them didn't, some vital clue. "I'm not asking for myself but for Jessie. She's in terrible danger, and I want to know how to help her."

Dr. Stieveson turned away.

"Dad!" Nick put his hand on his father's arm.

"I read your notes. I know about Marina and what she is. We need to talk."

His father shook his head. "You don't know everything. You think you do — but you don't." He grimaced with pain.

"I want to know more. I want — I want to know everything."

"Then feast your eyes on this." His father hurled down his beer can and started to take off his shoe. It was almost impossible to wedge off his foot, which was incredibly swollen. Then he had to peel down his sock, inch by painful inch until finally his foot was bare. His toes had started to grow together so that the lines were not even visible except the fork between the big toe and all the rest.

"What happened? Is it some sort of rare disease?" Nick was astounded.

"It's your Marina," his father spat. "She still doesn't have a pulse and she walks around. She knows I know and holds me in contempt. She is certain I won't dare tell anybody because they'll think I'm crazy. But just to make sure she started to turn me into a pig. I think that's the beginning of a pig's foot — a hoof."

For a long time Nick and his father stared at each other and at the horrible deformation.

Nick felt faintly nauseated. "I know about the family curse and all, but this is wild."

"All you know is a story I told you as a child. She's even more dangerous than you think."

His father then told him how every generation since 1897 a member of the Stieveson family had died violently by the sea. It was usually a woman, a Stieveson's wife or sweetheart just like Anna the fisherman's daughter. It seemed that Ingrid the witch hunted them down to make certain that the descendants of Captain Stieveson were no happier in love than he had been with his Anna.

Of course the twentieth-century Stievesons had been descended from Anna's little boy, the one she had left behind with a cold that fatal night she had drowned. She had called him "Olaf Stieveson" after her lover, and Olaf he remained. Ingrid's first attack didn't occur until he was a grown man and married many years, living in the Stieveson house on the oceanfront. His wife was Nick's great-grandmother. Her husband, Olaf, had warned her never to go near the sea no matter what she saw. She wasn't to go there even to swim, and she had obeyed him. Ingrid had tried many tricks to lure her there, but the woman had turned a deaf ear to the witch.

Instead Lady Ingrid haunted her. She made the woman deathly afraid of water, and not just seawater. Ingrid's face appeared staring up at her from the water in every sink, every bucket, every bathtub, and finally every drinking cup. One day the old woman was having tea. She dropped the china cup, startled to see the witch's image staring up at her from the bottom of the cup. No matter how she washed and scrubbed it, the face would not fade.

The woman became afraid of bathing, scrubbing, and in the end even drinking water. The poor lady went mad, refusing all food and water and starving herself. In the last days of her life it was said she kept her eyes shut all the time to avoid seeing Ingrid.

A generation later, the wife of the next Stieveson, Nick's grandmother, heard a child out at sea calling for help. The cry would stop every time the old lady searched through the spyglass upstairs. Nick's grandfather tried to prevent his wife from going to the rescue, knowing what her end would be. But the sound of the child's wailing never stopped day or night.

Nick's grandmother went out on the beach early one morning when her husband was still asleep. She was determined to put an end to the crying once and for all. But no sooner did she put one foot in the surf than a giant wave smashed ashore. In its swirling waters rose the smiling face of Lady Ingrid. Just as it swallowed her up and drowned her, her husband cried out. He had seen it all and been unable to stop it. Her body was washed up on shore. No child's corpse was ever found.

"But, Dad." Nick sat on the edge of his chair. "What about mother? Is she safe?"

Nick's father looked at him sadly. "She's perfectly safe. It's time you knew. Your mother isn't the woman who gave birth to you."

So that was why people had always said his sisters looked so different from him. Nick was shocked and took the news silently. His father gave him time and suffered quietly with him.

"My second wife adopted you at three months. But since we didn't live here in Virginia Beach at the time, few people knew you weren't her natural son when we moved back. We lived in Tucson, Arizona. I remained there one month after my first wife, your mother, died."

"But, Dad, I thought the Stievesons had always lived in this house."

"I was born here," his father said. "I knew

about the curse. My father told me long before I married. So I tried to head it off with that scientific brain of mine! Curse my logical mind! I thought that nothing could happen if we moved away from here and left the sea behind. I got a job at the University of Arizona in Tucson way out there in the desert. There were no oceans for hundreds of miles. I congratulated myself that we were safe."

"You weren't?"

"I'd explained the curse to your mother carefully, but she was a scientist and laughed it off as an old wives' tale. After she gave birth to you she arranged one day without my knowledge to leave you in the care of friends — just like Anna of old. She and some women from the university drove to the beach in Mexico on the Pacific Coast. She was sunning herself and went into the water to wet herself in the waves, not even to swim. Her horrified friends testified later that by the time they heard her scream it was too late. She came running out of the surf with the tentacles of a jellyfish clinging to her legs. She tried to rip off the sticky threads. Her friends helped her, but it was no use. She turned blue, collapsed, and died on the beach within minutes even before they could summon a doctor. The physician who performed the autopsy said that such a jellyfish, the sea wasp, had never been found so close to the west coast of North America before. They normally inhabit only Australian waters."

In a moment of silence Nick remembered Ingrid's ability to change herself and others into animals and horrible creatures. She had changed into the sea wasp that killed his mother. He now had another reason to hate her. "Wait until I get my hands on this Marina . . . Ingrid . . . whatever she calls herself!" Nick vowed.

"This is the girl." His father showed him one of his great-grandmother's old teacups with the face imprinted on the bottom. Nick stared at the image looking back at him. There was that simpering face of blond hair and china-white skin. And those blue eyes of mockery seemed to blaze out at him even now, boasting her course of destruction through all those generations. Nick hurled the cup to the ground and watched it shatter.

It was the same girl all right. Still, the mystery of Jessie's involvement remained. It was even stranger now than before. His father's story had only intensified the questions. Jessie was not a Stieveson. She was his girlfriend, but they were not married or even engaged. Above all, why didn't Marina kill Jessie as she had killed all the other women in the Stievesons' past? She certainly held Jessie in her absolute power. Yet Marina did nothing but court and court, lure and lure, as if Jessie were somehow different from all the rest, different from other people altogether — and very, very important.

"Dad, Marina doesn't mean to kill Jessie. I'm sure of that now. What is she up to?"

"I'm afraid I can't help you there, son." His father clapped him on the shoulder and turned away to his beer can and the television set. "It seems she's up to something we can't even imagine."

They had talked late into the night and into the wee hours of the morning. Nick dozed off in the chair where he had sat listening to his family's story. It seemed that he had been asleep only a few moments when the ringing phone woke him. He groped for the receiver and finally got hold of it. As he opened his eyes he saw that it was morning. It was Saturday, the day of the big end-of-the-year swim meet. It was raining outside.

"Hello."

"Nick, it's Trish."

"Are you still in the car?"

"Yes, but you've got to hurry. Jessie's gone."

"What?" Nick stood up, fully awake now. "Where did she go?"

"Marina spent the night at her house. The two of them just got into her old Buick and drove down the road. We're just out of sight around the corner."

"Follow them!" Nick said, waiting breathlessly as he listened to the Cadillac's engine rev up. He gave Trish and Dot a few minutes to get under way and tail the Buick. Then he said, "Where are they going?"

"Who knows?" said Trish. "But they just got into the lane headed for the beach."

Chapter 9

Dear Diary:

I haven't talked to you for a long time now, Diary. But with everything else going on it's easy to forget — except when I feel like this.

Wretched's the word. When I'm around Marina, I'm on top of the world. I'm going to become the next Olympic gold medalist in swimming. Nothing can possibly go wrong.

But Nick is a real downer. Earlier today Marina and I were doing math homework in the living room, or at least we were making a show of it. Really she was telling me about how we would enter all the swimming meets next season and how it was all just the beginning. I was already starting to see myself on television. Suddenly Nick popped up out of the blue. He looked horrible, so scared that I sat bolt upright. What's wrong with him? I thought. There must be something wrong. Am I so stupid that I don't see it?

For the first time I really noticed the look she gave Nick when she thought I wasn't watching her. It was enough to give me nightmares. Her pretty face and smooth features were all screwed up with hate.

Nick stared at her as if he would strangle her with those big hands of his. His fingers were even twitching. He couldn't seem to keep them still in her presence. He was doing everything he could to get me to come with him and leave Marina behind.

Marina is my best friend, but yes, I still love Nick. I guess he's sort of become my boyfriend. I wish they wouldn't argue like this and tear me apart. That's what I feel like — a paper doll that each is tugging from a different end. I just want to scream.

I was afraid to go with Nick because of what she might do to him or he to her. So I just played dumb and told Nick, "I'm busy. I've got a test Monday."

That made Marina very happy. She reached over and patted my shoulder. For the first time I can remember, I trembled all over. I wanted to move away, but I didn't.

She invited herself to stay here tonight.

Strange, but I don't really want her to stay. She's a good talker and she keeps my mind off the meet, but I can't help staring at those long, slender white fingers. I keep noticing that one eye of hers seems brighter than the other. I don't mind saying it's more than a little frightening. I want to get to sleep to shake off this strange mood. I hope that's all it is.

It was the Saturday of the big swim meet, the last one of the year. It would determine who would take home the top prizes and awards. That was Jessie's first conscious thought when she woke up.

The thought seemed to grab her by the stomach and tighten its hold. Outside it was pouring down rain and was one of the gloomiest days she'd seen all spring. The meet wasn't until late that afternoon at the high school's indoor pool.

Jessie looked at the silent form of Marina, who was sleeping in the cot on the far side of the room. Her new friend seemed so calm in sleep, so harmless. At least she *thought* Marina was still her friend.

"Good morning!" Marina stretched lazily like a cat and sat up.

"I think I'm going to die." Jessie put her

hand to her stomach and stared out at the rain. It was coming down in sheets now.

"Nonsense," Marina said. "I've got a treat in store." She clapped her hands together. "Take your mind off your breaststroke a little. Why don't we go to the beach and do a little surfing? Get limbered up."

"But it's raining!" Jessie protested. It was rare she objected to anything that Marina said. But this was so obvious. How could they possibly go swimming or surfing in weather like this?

"Don't worry," Marina shrugged. "It's just a thunderstorm. It will pass soon." Marina was always so confident of everything she said. It was as if she weren't just making a prediction — she knew. Jessie felt envious of her confidence, but she could not shake her feeling of unease.

Marina turned her gaze on her friend. Jessie felt something scorch right through her.

"All right," Jessie finally conceded. "I'm game. Let me ask Mom for the car keys."

But Jessie was back only moments later. "Sorry, Marina. It's no go. Mom says she needs the car herself. Her car's in the shop today." For some reason that news almost made Jessie feel cheerful.

Even this did not perturb Marina. Nor did

it change her plans. "Let me speak to your mom," she said. Marina tossed her blond locks over her shoulder and walked into the kitchen with the poise of a beauty queen.

Jessie bet on her mom, but Marina returned with the keys and a bright smile. "Everything's settled. Hop in. Let's get going."

Jessie climbed into the driver's seat in the pouring rainstorm. Marina looked at her and said, "Scoot over. I'm going to drive." Jessie was being dispossessed of her own car. It might not be much of a car, but at least it had been hers.

For the first time since the day Jessie met Marina, she was beginning to get a feeling of panic. Her mother never gave in that easily, especially when matters of principle were involved. How had Marina gotten her to change her mind?

Jessie did not know what to feel — joy, elation, relief, suspicion, or dread. So she felt numb while Marina revved up the car and started down Great Neck Road. It was almost as if she didn't dare breathe. She had the distinct feeling that something was about to happen as the windshield wipers flicked back and forth. She hardly listened as Marina chatted on and on about the beach.

In the side-view mirror on the passenger side she caught sight of another car rapidly approaching them from behind. It was a red Lincoln Town Car. It looked like Mrs. Stieveson's car, the one Jessie always saw parked outside the ladies' clubs, fancy clothing boutiques in Norfolk, and hair salons all over town.

But when Jessie looked hard she couldn't see Mrs. Stieveson with her towering blond updo. It was Nick! She would recognize that red hair anywhere. He was gripping the steering wheel with one hand and driving with his cast on. He had an intent look on his face, and he seemed to be staring straight at her. He started to honk his horn and got closer and closer until he was almost riding on their bumper.

"What a bore!" sighed Marina. "Doesn't that boy *ever* give up?" she suddenly said like someone much older than seventeen. The lines around her lips curled downward and tiny wrinkles appeared about her eyes, giving her an older, more worldly appearance of disgust and boredom.

"Marina, what's happening?" Jessie stared at her aghast. "You're changing."

"Don't we all, dear. Don't we all . . ." Marina was concentrating on the sight of Nick in her rearview mirror. "Well, let's give him a run for his money."

She smashed her foot down on the gas pedal, and the car lurched forward on the rain-slick streets. The Buick might not be a sports car, but Marina exacted every ounce of acceleration from its old, tired engine. Jessie wondered if she had put more than gasoline into it. She had put her will into it.

Jessie never knew how Marina managed to avoid the station wagon in front of them. She turned the steering wheel sharply and jumped out of the right-hand lane into the passing lane on the Virginia Beach Expressway. She wove in and out of traffic, trucks and cars alike, accelerating to speeds of over seventy miles an hour. Then the speedometer began to climb to eighty.

Marina was trying to avoid Nick, but Jessie wondered if she didn't have something more tricky in mind. She must have seen he had only one hand on the wheel. Was she attempting to outmaneuver him and get him to crash? Jessie felt positive of it. It seemed she could read Marina's mind.

"Don't you think we ought to stop and at least hear what Nick has to say?" Jessie dared to ask.

"Bad habits die hard, don't they, Jessie?" Marina turned her vivid blue eyes on her. Jessie saw what she wasn't supposed to see. The lines around Marina's mouth were cold and hard. She was even suddenly aware that Marina expected her gaze to subdue her as it always did.

Jessie turned away from the stranger, her heart pounding in fright.

"Don't be afraid, dear." Marina put her hand on Jessie's. "Just relax and pretend you're having the time of your life. There's no danger involved here, not when you're riding with Marina."

Jessie held onto the seat and prayed silently, *Dear God, please don't let Nick get killed!*

Nick did not let Marina stay in front of him for long. He cut her off on more than one occasion, forcing her back into the right lane. Their cars bumped against each other, side against side, making Jessie feel as if she were about to fly out the door with each impact. Nick leaned across the front seat of his car and called out the window, "Jessie! Jessie! You've got to listen to me!"

Jessie turned away. She dared not look at him for fear of what Marina might do.

Marina exited off the expressway and

headed for Pacific Avenue. They lost sight of Nick for a few minutes, and Jessie dared to hope he was safe. Then he suddenly thrust his car in front of them from a side lane, just as a police car did when it wanted to stop another vehicle at any cost.

Instead of hitting the brakes, Marina curled her lips into a maniacal grin. She stomped down on the gas pedal.

"No!" screamed Jessie. "You're going to kill him." She tried to grab the steering wheel from Marina.

But Marina had arms of steel. She held the steering wheel in a vise. Just before the impact, the girl looked at her. There was no fear at all in her eyes, only great satisfaction.

The Buick smashed into the side of Nick's car. The Lincoln skidded but didn't flip over, though it rocked dangerously. A deep "V" dent was cut into the door on the passenger side.

Nick leaped out of his car in no time, yanking Jessie out of her seat. Marina did all but grab her other arm. "Jessie, stay here!" Marina barked in an uncharacteristically nasty voice. "I mean you don't need to get out," she quickly changed her tone.

It did no good. Jessie was already facing Nick, his big hands gripping her by the shoulders, shaking her. "Wake up, Jess!" he pleaded. "She's not Marina Jacobsen any more than I'm George Washington. She's not really alive anymore, Jess. She's dead and she's after you."

In a moment of blinding panic, it all came back to her. She remembered the story Nick had told her about his ancestors and the woman called "Lady Ingrid." The wild blonde hair, the blazing turquoise eyes, the power to kill . . . Ingrid was Marina, and Marina was Ingrid. That's why the girl hated Nick. But why she was caught in the middle she had no idea. All she knew was she had to save Nick. She would protect him with her last remaining bit of strength.

Jessie had to act. She was conscious of Marina's eyes on her, burning into her. She pretended to scoff, "What nonsense, Nick! Are you sick or something? Maybe your brain should be in a cast instead of your arm." Jessie tried her best to laugh. Marina joined her, sounding thoroughly wicked. "Go home, Nick." Jessie thrust him away, hoping to keep him alive.

Every limb was trembling as Jessie got back into the Buick and drove on with Marina. It took every ounce of courage she had to slam that car door. Despite the Buick's smashed-in front end Jessie knew the car would drive. Marina would make sure of it.

The rain cascaded down in torrents. Nick slogged his lonely way home through the puddles with the Lincoln's windshield wipers working full blast. The collision with the Buick had punched a huge dent in the car's righthand side, but it was still drivable.

It all seemed hopeless. He had lost Jessie to that creature.

Nick was so despondent he was not paying much attention to where he was headed. He ignored the signs. He didn't notice the traffic thinning out as he passed by his house and headed beyond the end of Atlantic Avenue to Shore Drive. He didn't hear the friendly lady who rolled down her window in the blinding rain and called to him, "The road's washed out ahead, son! Turn back. Try a different route!"

A few minutes later Nick entered a standing puddle of water on the road that was deeper than it looked. It was too late by the time he felt his tires leave the pavement. By then he had lost all power to steer his car. He felt the Lincoln being carried away, swept downstream into a swamp by Seashore State Park.

Nick saw the black water coming before the car hit it and started to sink.

"Jess!" he cried out. "Jess, help!"

Jessie thought she heard a cry, but she shrugged it off. She and Marina had just entered the parking lot beside the Norwegian Lady monument. As Marina had predicted, the rain had ended abruptly and the sun was coming out.

Jessie could hardly meet Marina's gaze, she was so paralyzed with fear. Yet even in her panic she showed courage. "Marina, maybe we ought to go back and look for Nick. He was awfully upset. After all I am supposed to be his friend, too."

"You disappoint me when you talk like that. You'll never get anywhere." All sympathy was gone from her voice. She sounded as cold as ice.

Jessie watched silently as Marina took the surfboards down from the roof rack of the car. Jessie pretended to listen while Marina gave her pointers. But her mind was really on Nick. Jessie was thinking, *I don't care what you do with me. Just leave him alone.*

Jessie went out on the surfboard, but her worries about Nick started blocking her skill to stay on the board. Even Marina noticed. All of a sudden there was something more than her simple worries. It was a premonition that a dreadful accident had happened. Soon it became a certainty.

A picture of Nick with black water all around him flashed across her mind. It was pressing in on his lungs and crushing the air out of them. For the first time while awake and for the first time in many days, Jessie felt the dark something pressing in on her lungs. As she gasped for breath and fell off the board, she thought, *Why didn't I know it until now? All these weeks I've been seeing Nick's death and I couldn't stop it. Nick!*

A hard object struck her on the head. Everything went black.

"I have to find Nick," Jessie was mumbling as she opened her eyes. Faces she didn't recognize were standing over her as she lay on her back in the sand.

"Are you all right?" said a girl. "That looks like a nasty bump."

Marina cut her way through the crowd. "Come on, Jessie, let's get going." Her voice was dry and unsympathetic. "We'll be late for the swim meet."

"But . . ." Jessie sat up, rubbing her head. The lump on her head was very sore. "I don't think I'll be swimming today."

"What do you mean? This is your best chance!" Marina grabbed her by the hand and pulled her to her feet. She seemed to be in a big hurry, as if she were afraid Jessie might change her mind or something.

In the car Jessie could not help looking at Marina in undisguised horror. She almost asked, "What do you want from me?"

"Come on, I'm on your side." Marina patted Jessie's cheek. "Let's perk up." She gave Jessie a dazzling smile. Her smile almost seemed as warm as old times. But it was too late. Jessie was beginning to see Marina in a strange new light.

Marina had not let her die in the surf. In fact, Marina had been the one to save her and pull her up on shore. She did not seem to want her death. What could she possibly want — what evil thing? And what did it have to do with the swim meet?

Marina kept telling her, "You're a great swimmer, Jess. You're going to come in first. Then it's to the state competition in Richmond, the regionals, and the nationals. Who knows after that. . . . You and I will be quite a team, won't we?"

Jessie heard nothing. Thoughts of Nick blocked out all of Marina's crazy ambitions. He was hurt, and he needed her. He wasn't dead yet. She would know when he was gone. Jessie did not dare ask herself how she knew these things. She was living by her premonitions, which grew stronger by the minute.

Somehow Marina managed to get Jessie to the locker room and into her swimsuit. Then she hustled Jessie down to the pool. Jessie stood on the starting box, ready for her first event. All she could see was Marina's smiling face, sitting on the bench with the other coaches and teachers. No one questioned Marina's right to be there.

But Jessie sensed that something was about to happen more terrible than anything yet. Again, she was overcome by a crippling sensation of powerlessness.

Suddenly she spotted Trish and Dot in the balcony waving at her. Trish stuck out from the crowd in her striped jeans and polka dot shirt. The girls didn't look as if they'd come to watch the swim meet. Worry was written all over their faces. Dot was rubbing her eyes as if she'd been crying. They were trying to signal her.

The shrill whistle cut through Jessie like a knife. Her legs were taught to respond automatically, and she dove forward into the water. The wet hit her in the face before she knew it. But with every stroke she felt more and more anxious. She couldn't swim anymore. Her legs froze. Her arms wouldn't respond. She popped her head up from the water as the other swimmers flashed past her. Trish and Dot were holding up a cardboard sign amidst all the cheering students in the stands. "It's Nick," the words said.

That was all Jessie needed to know. She sprang out of the pool. Marina was calling to her, but she didn't listen. She dashed through the locker rooms without even stopping for her clothes. Trish and Dot were waiting at the exit. They threw a towel around her shoulders, and they all headed straight for the car.

Trish and Dot had thought of everything. The girls had brought an old pair of jeans and a sweatshirt for Jessie to put on while she was riding. "Nick's been injured again — badly this time," Dot turned around from the front seat and blurted out. She was wiping away tears with a Kleenex.

"Where is he?" Jessie willed the car to move faster. As if she could read Jessie's mind, Trish pushed the gas pedal to the floor.

"Norfolk Memorial Hospital," Dot sobbed.

There was the unanswered question lingering in the air that no one dared ask or answer. Finally Dot continued to weep and even Trish, solid Trish, could not help but cry. Jessie knew it must be bad, very bad. Trish said, "Nick's dying, Jess. I'm sorry, but I've got to tell you. He's unconscious. They've got him on life support."

In her mind Jessie felt the impact of car hitting car again. She saw Marina's malicious look. *I can't let this continue, not when it means Nick's life,* Jessie thought to herself as if she had the power to stop it. "What happened?" She sat forward in the backseat.

"He was driving back from the beach and got caught in the thunderstorm. He must not have been paying much attention to where he was going. He drove down a flooded street, and his car got washed away. He hit his head and nearly drowned — right in his car!"

Jessie would not cry. That would be admitting that Nick would die. Nick would not die. She wouldn't let him.

Nick's mother and sisters were with him in

175

the hospital room. The nurse told Jessie it was family only at this point. She was sorry, but his friends from school could not be admitted.

"Let me see him!" Jessie said. She stared at the woman very hard. A certain power she had never felt before came to her aid. The nurse seemed to back off and showed her the way to Nick's room, unable to take her eyes from Jessie's face.

The hospital staff did nothing to stop Jessie, though Trish and Dot had to stay in the waiting room. Jessie did not even look at Nick's weeping mother or his sisters. She went straight to his bed where he was hidden under an oxygen tent with all sorts of tubes coming and going from his arms and neck. They didn't deter her. She moved them gently to the side and grabbed for his hand. His mother and sisters were too grief-stricken to stop her.

"Nick!" she commanded him. "Nick, listen to me. You've got to live. You've got to pull out of this. Look at me." She felt a strength welling up in her that she never guessed she possessed before. Ordinary, plain Jessie was not ordinary or plain anymore. Where her hand met his cold one, she felt a certain heat start up. She rubbed his hand and spoke soothingly to him until he stirred and turned his head toward her. He even opened his eyes and gazed into hers.

"Jess!" he whispered her name. His lips curled upward into a faint smile. He reached out to touch a lock of brown hair.

Now Jessie knew who she was or rather what she was. She had always thought herself peculiar. She constantly daydreamed and had experienced premonitions and nightmares all her life. Now it was all explained. Now she knew why Marina wanted to lure her into traps. Now she knew why Marina did not just kill her.

She could not.

Marina had felt from the first that she, Jessie, had the same power as Marina. She probably meant to entrap Jessie just as she had trapped poor Captain Stieveson — but before Jessie found out what she was. Then Marina meant to have her soul. No doubt at that point, Jessie would lose her own powers and belong to Marina. Marina would be the only one with power.

But who was she? Who was Jessie Rogers? Why did she have the power? Where did she get it? Those questions eluded her as much as always.

"Well, hello, daughter," said Marina, startling her. Jessie looked up to gaze into the other girl's turquoise-blue eyes. But now she didn't back away. Jessie met her eye for eye.

It was Marina who led Jessie back to the Stieveson house and told her the rest of the story. Jessie was indeed the descendant of Lady Ingrid's and Captain Stieveson's only daughter, the one they had left behind in Norway when they came to America on *The Norwegian Lady*. Neither Jessie's great-grandmother nor her grandmother wanted to cooperate with the Lady Ingrid. Each one wanted ordinary happiness, the happiness of mortals.

Jessie's mother turned out to be the most disappointing of all, as a dreary old school-teacher in a dreary, middle-class high school in Virginia Beach. Mrs. Rogers wanted nothing to do with magic and tried to stamp out her own daughter's "worst tendencies" for fear she would succumb.

In a moment of insight Jessie now understood her mother as never before. She saw why it upset her when her daughter day-dreamed and didn't pay attention. Her mother knew what was coming and the price her daughter would have to pay. That was why she warned Jessie away from Nick and the Stievesons after trouble started.

Her mother had recognized Marina from the beginning. That's why she'd acted so frightened, ordering her daughter away from the new girl, but at the same time she was afraid to disobey Marina's wishes. That's also why her mother had given Marina the car keys she had refused to Jessie.

"What about the pool and all that Olympic stuff?" Jessie said suspiciously.

Marina shrugged. "I wanted to show you how great your powers are. You can have anything you want."

"Didn't you try to drown me that first day when I saw you surfing?" Jessie asked.

"No way!" smiled Marina. "I wanted to show you that you could be immortal like me. Those boys drowned by the old pier in April. They found my crystal and tried to steal it so I took care of them. But you're like me, remember? You *can't* drown."

Much depended upon what Jessie decided now. Sagely, she waited for Marina — Lady Ingrid — to take the lead. The story of the boys by the old pier had given her an idea. They hadn't died in vain. Jessie would see to that.

"Don't be a fool, join me!" Marina said. "I'll show you a world of wonders you can't imagine. We don't need anyone. We can take what people have to offer and then get rid of them. You don't need to be sweet on this Nick."

"Gee, I thought he would be the only boyfriend I would ever have!" Jessie played along, but she was working on a plan. "I can't believe how powerful we are." She looked into Marina's eyes and could now tell for sure that the right one was the crystal eye with the blue turquoise center. The one where the soul of Captain Stieveson was imprisoned. "Do you mean I could have one, too, a crystal eye I mean?"

"Certainly. Let me show you how." Marina reached for Jessie's right eye.

Jessie jerked away at the last moment.

A look of suspicion came over Marina's face.

"I'm not quite ready yet. Can't I use yours for now, just to see how it works?" Jessie tried to cover up for her nervousness.

Marina smiled. This was pure delight to her, even child's play. She'd been waiting so long to have a partner in crime. Marina spent the rest of the afternoon instructing her great-great-granddaughter in all her tricks. She even laid her hands on Jessie's shoulders and imbued her with all of her supernatural powers.

Jessie felt the warmth penetrating throughout her body, even to the core of her bones. She felt herself growing and expanding in spirit until she took in the sun and the moon, the stars in the sky, and the whole earth and sea beneath. Her powers were infinite. She could see into the hearts and minds of every person. It was an awesome strength. But unlike Ingrid, unlike Marina, she would be careful. She would use her gift for the good. She would save Nick and those she loved from harm or her name wasn't Jessie Rogers.

Chapter 10

A week after Nick's miraculous recovery, Jessie and Marina picked up him, Trish, and Dot in the Buick. The car had been to the shop for some body work and looked almost as good as new. Marina said that her parents had come to claim her at last. She was supposed to drive to the Norfolk Airport to meet them, and she wanted all her "friends" to come along.

"Gee, Marina, it's about time," said Dot, looking uncomfortable. No one knew why Marina was suddenly being nice to them. She'd always shunned them before.

"Who are your parents?" said the more practical Trish, looking skeptical.

"You'll never guess," Marina beamed at them. "I want it to be my surprise."

Trish and Dot looked at each other with sickly smiles. They shifted in their seats.

Jessie said nothing. She merely turned her adoring eyes on Marina and nodded her head, all agreement. It was all planned. Jessie had her part, and Marina had hers. Marina had agreed to help Jessie capture Nick the way she, as Lady Ingrid, had captured Captain Stieveson. Jessie was to possess Nick's soul forever. Nick was to be changed from a boy she had known and admired all her life into her slave.

That was if Marina had her way. Jessie had bet her life Marina would not. She tensed to prepare herself to carry out her plan. If she faltered once, all would be lost. She might lose Nick forever.

Nick stared at Jessie. Jessie knew he was trying to get her to meet his gaze. No doubt he had not forgotten that he had opened his eyes and found her standing over him. Perhaps he sensed a new Jessie. But he could not guess just how different.

If all went well, Jessie promised herself she would make it up to Nick later.

Jessie was grateful for one piece of luck as she smiled at Marina. The witch, was so wrapped up in her evil designs that she could not detect Jessie's pounding heartbeat.

Marina seemed to be perfectly content. She

had no joy except to torment the Stieveson family. This was her ultimate revenge. Nick had no brothers, and his sisters would marry and take other names. Nick had not married, nor did he have children. When he died, the Stieveson name would come to an untimely end.

At the airport Marina went to the ticket counter to ask about the flight. Of course she came back with the information that the flight was delayed.

"Why don't we go to the Norfolk Botanical Gardens?" Jessie remembered her line. "They're right next door." She smiled at Marina, and the two exchanged looks as if they shared secrets. Jessie fawned on her. She didn't want Marina to suspect anything. Not when there was so little time left.

"Gee, Jess, it looks like everybody else is leaving," Dot said as they pulled into the parking lot at the gardens.

"I don't blame them," snorted Trish. "It's clouding up and getting windy."

But nothing could stop Marina. Jessie followed right behind, biding her time.

After buying their tickets they walked around a little, looking at the gorgeous displays of rhododendrons as tall as trees with pink, white, and red May blossoms as big as a fist. Or, as Marina said, "As big as a human heart."

"My legs are getting tired," said Jessie quite casually but again according to plan. She remembered to signal Marina with her eyes. None of this exchange was lost on Nick. He tried to take Jessie's hand, but she pulled away from him. It pained her to see his crushed, uncomprehending expression. She had to be cruel now so she could be kind later.

Dot and Trish stared at Jessie openly in amazement. They whispered to Nick while Marina excused herself to freshen up.

"All right, Jess, what's the trick?" Trish finally said. "Whose side are you on?"

She must be doing a good job of acting if she could fool Nick, Trish, and Dot. "I don't know what you mean." She played dumb.

"I thought you knew about Marina," whispered Dot. "Now you two seem to be better friends than ever."

"We are better friends than ever," Jessie said in case Marina was listening.

"Shall we stand in line for the boats?" Marina smoothed her hair down with her comb as she returned from the ladies' room. Of course Jessie sensed that she hadn't been to the ladies' room at all. Marina had been merely watching her with her friends.

Nick grabbed Jessie's arm and plowed on through the crowd toward the boats. Nick stuck to her side stubbornly no matter what. Poor, dear Nick. . . . Jessie wanted to alert him to run for his life. This was going to get far more dangerous before it was all over. She imagined him as a shriveled up creature imprisoned in the turquoise center of a crystal, and she shook all over. Death was better than that. She would kill him first.

"Do you really think we ought to go out on the water?" asked Trish as they paid their money. She glanced up at the darkening sky. "It looks like the storm's about here."

"If Jessie goes, I'm going," said Nick, gloomily sticking his one good hand into his pocket. He was still all bandaged up. His arm still hung in a sling. Jessie wanted desperately to reach out and hug him.

Theirs was the last boat to leave the dock for the tour through the canals and out to the bay that joined with the Atlantic Ocean. They were the only passengers. The other tourists opted for the train ride. They didn't want to be out on the bay when that big black cloud gathering overhead broke.

Jessie and Nick sat behind Marina, Dot, and Trish. Marina chose the seat nearest the water. As the tour boat wound through the canals, the guide pointed out the Colonial Garden, the Rose Garden, the Japanese Garden, and the azaleas. Long tendrils from weeping willow trees reached down and brushed against them, entangling the group in their vines. Jessie felt the vines were warning them — holding them back.

Marina was childish in her delight for the water. She leaned way over the side, dipping her hand in the murky green depths, letting it brush against the vines and the reeds growing on the banks. The tour guide told her to keep her hands in the boat — that was until Marina turned and stared at him fixedly.

Jessie kept her gaze fixed on Marina's eye, the crystal one with the turquoise center.

When they reached the bay, Nick let his good arm slip around Jessie's waist and tried to hug her to him. He squeezed her even harder when she squirmed away. Then he whispered, "Jessie! What's wrong? Why won't you look at me?"

She would not respond, though her heart did flip-flops. She was terrified that Marina would see them together and begin to suspect.

Perhaps it was just as well this way. Nick had given her an out without even knowing it. She had wondered until now how else she was going to perform her part. "How dare you!" She smacked Nick in the face. "Keep your hands off me." She stood up in the boat. The boat rocked dangerously.

"Get down!" yelled the tour guide just as the first thunderbolt crackled in the sky and lightning flashed. "We've got to turn back."

"Jessie, what's wrong with you?" Nick wrestled her down. "We'll capsize!"

Before they knew it, the boat went over. Nick and Jessie thrashed about in the turbulent water. The tour guide, Trish, and Dot barely made it to shore.

"Now!" screamed Marina. "Do it now. Make him bargain for his life, for his soul, and then you'll have him." Marina was nearly panting with eagerness, her face a plaster cast of hate.

Marina raised her arms and brought them crashing down against the water, making the waves grow higher in the howling wind. She kept her eyes intently fixed on Jessie and Nick as if about to partake of a great feast.

"Lend me your turquoise eye . . . you promised!" Jessie yelled to her at the top of her lungs to be heard over the thunder. "I don't know quite how to use my own yet."

Concentrating only on her revenge, Marina quickly complied. She plucked out her right eye and handed it carefully to Jessie. To the witch this crystal eye was worth all the gold and jewels in the world, for it held imprisoned the soul of Captain Stieveson. Soon it would hold Nick as well. She would not even have to give him back to Jessie later if she didn't want to.

Jessie again held the crystal eye. Captain Stieveson's voice cried, *"Help! Jessie, help! It's been so long. Please set me free."*

"Soon," she promised in a whisper.

Jessie turned to Nick, who treaded water with the most stoic expression. He was having a hard time keeping his head up because of his cracked ribs and the cast. His breaststroke did him no good now. He looked betrayed, hurt, but willing to accept what fate had in store. He said, "Jessie, how can you do this? I'm not like Captain Stieveson. I didn't betray you. I love you. No matter what you do to me I still will."

Then, counting to ten, as she raised the eye above her and put all the force of her power into it, Jessie whipped around in the water and faced Marina instead. "Release Captain Stieveson!" Jessie commanded in a booming voice that sounded louder and deeper than her own. "Release him or you die!"

Marina cried out in pain. "You're killing me. I can't see. You're blinding me." A brilliant white light flooded out from the eye, irradiating the witch struggling in the lake. "*Ah-h-h-h-h!* You little traitor. I'll kill you for this."

"You no longer have the power. I do!" Jessie said.

For the last time they stared at each other eye-to-eye. Marina tore out her hair in fury at this betrayal. Great chunks of blond flax came out and floated on the waters. "What can those poor mortals give you that I cannot? What is that boy to immortal life and everlasting power?"

"Nick loves me, and I love him. You don't love anybody."

"But you don't know all the secrets yet!" Marina began to shrivel.

"And I don't care," said Jessie.

The evil witch fought back with all her art. She tried to terrify Jessie into dropping the crystal eye by changing herself into every form imaginable from ferocious animals and sea creatures to horrible, terrifying faces. Nothing helped. She was dying.

"Release Captain Stieveson, and I'll drop this eye." Jessie took pity on her.

"Never!" gasped Marina with her last breath. She had turned into a shriveled gray form, no longer recognizable as human.

In a flash of light so blinding and brilliant that not even Jessie could look upon it, the witch disappeared. A blue flame leaped upward from the turquoise center of the crystal and extinguished itself. The jewel suddenly felt lighter. The witch was dead, and Captain Stieveson had gone to his long-earned rest.

The storm had now blown itself out, and the waters were becoming calm again. Nick somehow managed to paddle over to Jessie. He kicked in place to keep himself afloat as he grabbed her with his good arm. Just before he embraced her, Jessie took the empty crystal orb and hurled it as far away from herself and her friends as she could.

"You've done it, Jess, you've done it," he said. "You've broken the curse."

A crowd was gathering on the shore. The freakishly violent storm and the boat accident at the park had been reported on all the local radio stations. Jessie's mother and father had both heard the shocking news, as had Nick's mom on her way home from picking up Nick's sisters at the mall. Dr. Stieveson, looking more like his old self, stood closest to the water. He held up his foot and smiled at Nick. Trish and Dot cheered for Jessie and Nick and everybody else applauded.

A police boat rescued the two as they floundered about in the lake, holding onto what was left of the boat and each other. As soon as they were ashore, Jessie embraced her mom with new affection. She whispered in her mother's ear that she now understood what she had suffered through all those years.

"Now I understand better myself," said Dr. Rogers, squeezing his wife's shoulder. "Your daughter's 'worst tendencies' have turned into her best ones." Her mother and father smiled at each other for the first time in a long while. They reached out for Jessie and hugged her to them.

The bay now slept in peace after the storm. Captain Stieveson and Anna could now rest.

Even Lady Ingrid had gone where she could create no more trouble, her revenge vanished with the thunder. This was once again a quiet spot with rosebushes brushing dogwoods and azaleas, weeping willows dragging their green tendrils in the murky swamp water. It was nothing more than a peaceful tidal basin where the sea met the land. All so very far away from the fjords of Norway.

The Norwegian Lady is still presiding over her plaza. She holds out her arms toward the far horizon and watches over all those men and women whose ships were taken by the sea.

About the Author

Linda Cargill is the author of several young adult horror and mystery novels, though *The Surfer* is her first for Scholastic. She, her husband, Gary, and her son, Kenny, like to load up their van and travel around the country every summer looking for story ideas and legends to make into novels for young people. Virginia Beach and Norfolk are real seafaring towns, full of stories of shipwrecks and legends about the sea.

Her son, Kenny, is her special consultant. He listens to every story and makes comments about it. He tells his mother what is interesting to kids and what isn't. He is especially good in a pinch when she can't think up a title.

Linda and her family live in Charlottesville, Virginia, with their three cats — Happy, Grumpy, and, of course, Spooky.

Terror is watching.

High on a hill,
trapped in the shadows,
something inside a dark house
is waiting...and watching.

THE HOUSE ON CHERRY STREET

**A three-book series
by Rodman Philbrick and Lynn Harnett**

Terror has a new home—and the children
are the only ones who sense it—from the
blasts of icy air in the driveway, to the windows
that shut like guillotines. Can Jason and Sally
stop the evil that lives in the dark?

**Book #1: THE HAUNTING
Book #2: THE HORROR
Book #3: THE FINAL NIGHTMARE**

HCS1194

NIGHTMARE HALL

where college is a scream!